HAZEL MAYES

Love at First Scratch

First published by Nine Lives Press 2026

Copyright © 2026 by Hazel Mayes

All rights reserved. No part of this publication may be reproduced, stored, or transmitted in any form or by any means, electronic, mechanical, photocopying, recording, scanning, or otherwise without written permission from the publisher. It is illegal to copy this book, post it to a website, or distribute it by any other means without permission.

This novel is entirely a work of fiction. The names, characters, and incidents portrayed in it are the work of the author's imagination. Any resemblance to actual persons, living or dead, events, or localities is entirely coincidental.

First edition

ISBN: 979-8-9878672-4-2

This book was professionally typeset on Reedsy. Find out more at reedsy.com

*To every stray cat who decided I was worth keeping—
Max, Cali, Charlie, Oliver, Maggie, Lila, Fred, Tommy,
and the nameless few who taught me love doesn't need a tag.*

*And to my husband, who passed his Cat Dad certification with
flying colors.*

Contents

Let's Talk Spice Level	iii
Nine Lives Club Rule #9	iv
Prologue	1
Chapter 1	6
Chapter 2	16
Chapter 3	26
Chapter 4	34
Chapter 5	38
Chapter 6	46
Chapter 7	53
Chapter 8	58
Chapter 9	63
Chapter 10	69
Chapter 11	76
Chapter 12	80
Chapter 13	84
Chapter 14	102
Chapter 15	107
Chapter 16	113
Chapter 17	119
Chapter 18	126
Chapter 19	133
Chapter 20	139
Chapter 21	146

Chapter 22	154
Chapter 23	159
Chapter 24	168
Chapter 25	179
Chapter 26	187
Epilogue	190
Before You Go ...	193
Soundtrack for Love at First Scratch	194
Cats Who Inspired the Story	195
Join the Series!	197
A Note from Hazel	198
Book Club Discussion Guide	199
About the Author	201
Also by Hazel Mayes	202

Let's Talk Spice Level

Whether you prefer to savor, skim, or skip the juicy bits, here's your quick guide to the heat in this story:

Spice Level: 3 (edging toward 4) — definitely open-door

Steamy chapters:
13
21
25

Nine Lives Club Rule #9

"You don't choose the cat—the cat chooses you."

Prologue

Ethan

Sunlight spilled across the green in front of City Hall as Ethan looked up from his book, just in time to see the librarian walking up to the front doors again.

His phone buzzed. He glanced down at, first, a photo of his slightly "chonky" orange tabby cat flopped on her back, paws kicking at a catnip toy stitched to look like a smiling avocado toast, then the name that flashed across. It was Carl, the foreman, already texting about plans for the next project. Ethan rolled his eyes. The man always did this—planting seeds about the crew's next move too far in advance. Sometimes it felt like Carl started talking about the next project the moment Ethan managed to update his address with the post office. He'd only been in Autumn Ridge for a few months, but the way Carl talked, you'd think their bags were already packed for the next job.

After a few years of this cycle, Ethan realized why he didn't like it. At first, Carl's communications had felt like job security. There was always another construction site that needed them. But now that Ethan was in his thirties, he wasn't so sure he liked feeling obligated to leave a place before he'd even had a chance to get to know it. Carl's reminders made him keep his distance from the locals, stay superficial, and never feel settled—just like his entire life had been up to this point. Moving had become second nature. Staying felt risky, like giving fate too big a target.

But Autumn Ridge was different. The town was working its way under his skin before he even realized it. He actually enjoyed the quiet pace and small-town predictability it offered—strong black coffee at Minka's Café, spotting Mayor Pennington on her early-morning jog, people remembering his name even when he wasn't sure he'd stayed long enough to deserve it. No one made fun of his old truck, and he'd even made a friend—Leo March, one of the firefighters—who'd come to Ethan's rescue after his cat climbed from the second-story balcony of his rented townhome into a nearby tree and got too scared to come back inside. He swore that had never happened before, and he appreciated Leo for not judging him for it or saying it was a waste of time. Ethan could certainly name a few cities they'd lived where that would have been the response.

A part of him kept saying he should just stick to what he knew and trusted. Don't get settled. Keep moving. Go where the work is. But there was something different here that drew him in and had been gnawing at the back of his head since he'd arrived.

Then one day Leo found himself stranded and needing the only toilet in his apartment repaired on short notice. It wasn't much to Ethan, just a toilet tank rebuild. Valve, flapper, flush valve—all of it had to come out. But they made kits for that kind of thing if you knew what you were doing. Still, Leo was impressed with how quickly Ethan got it fixed and asked him where he'd learned to do that. Ethan found himself telling Leo what his mother had always said about him—he was a guy who knew a little about a lot of things. The rest he could just figure out or find online.

To him, repairs were like cooking. Sometimes you had to figure it out as you went, testing along the way to reach the perfect result. Other times he knew that if he didn't follow the "recipe" step by step, it would never get fixed.

"Autumn Ridge needs a guy like that," Leo told him.

Next thing Ethan knew, he was getting calls from strangers who'd gotten his number from Leo, asking if he happened to know how to repair this or that. The construction site days were long, but this work felt different—personal, neighborly. He rebuilt mailboxes, fixed porch railings, and even figured out how to retrofit a pocket door into an existing wall. He appreciated the recognition and thanks he got from the people Leo sent his way, not to mention the autonomy. No Carl breathing down his neck. Sometimes the pay was great, too, and some people had even tipped on top of his fee. It got him thinking how, if he just found a way to make this handyman side hustle into a legitimate business, he might find a way to stay in Autumn Ridge. And as the thought became more tangible, he started thinking about the future in terms he'd never used before. *When the snow hits ... Next spring, I'll ...*

His mind pulled back to the quiet morning Carl had nearly ruined for him. The crew was scheduled to pack up by year's end, but Ethan wasn't sure he wanted to leave this time. He didn't reply to the text, choosing to savor his coffee and a few pages of his book before the day's dust and sweat arrived.

Then he saw her. Mauve cardigan and polka dot skirt, arms full of folders, waves of dark black hair that framed her long, slender neck. She looked like something out of a movie. She disappeared behind the library front doors and reappeared moments later with a bag in her hands. She knelt by the bushes near the steps and shook the bag. At first it looked like she was feeding squirrels, and then a gray cat slunk out from under the bench, followed by a second, and a third, and more, until she was surrounded.

He put his coffee down and leaned closer, peering across the street. She wasn't just feeding them. She was talking to them, sweetly, like they were old friends. She laughed when one of them pawed at her skirt, checked her watch but stayed for a few minutes longer anyway. Then she set down the rest of the food just far enough back for them to feel safe, offering up soft mewling noises as she slipped back inside.

The sight rooted him to the spot. The hammering in his chest didn't feel like attraction, even though that was there. It felt like recognition, like watching something right itself that had been off-balance for too long.

Ethan sat there for several minutes, in awe of what he had just witnessed and trying to pin down how it made him feel. It was like a light bulb switched on the moment he saw her. When she disappeared it started to fade, and he wanted that feeling back. He'd seen a lot of pretty women before. But like Autumn Ridge itself, this resident, likely a librarian, had suddenly thrown him off course.

He didn't see her for over a week after that. Against his better judgment, he got a library card. With all the travel, he'd been an avid e-book user since e-readers were invented. But visiting the library meant he just might catch another glimpse of the woman who'd been feeding the strays outside. Surely she was an employee.

Instead, a young librarian named Lucy, who seemed really flustered in his presence, took his information and got him set up with a library card. Ethan walked through the stacks, lingering, not only to pick out a few good books but also hoping he'd find the beautiful woman he'd seen open the library that day. A part of him wanted to ask Lucy if she knew who the woman was, but he was afraid that would be too obvious. He collected his books, checked them out, and thought of a plan as his truck puttered back to the row of townhomes.

He started getting his coffee earlier each workday just to figure out what time she arrived. He told himself it was nothing—just curiosity, just an attractive woman with a love for cats—until he was sitting at his favorite table, coffee steaming in his hand, and saw the mauve cardigan appear again. He smiled before he even realized it. But he didn't know what more he could do, despite narrowing in on her routine. He'd feel like an ass if he called out to her. From across the street no less. That's the kind of thing that could get him blacklisted by the library staff, and that was the last thing he wanted.

A few times, during breaks on the City Hall work, he glanced back at the library windows and caught light spilling across her silhouette as she arranged books inside. But she never seemed to look out the windows at the same time he was looking in.

He told himself it was fine. If he couldn't make this side gig into a business by year's end, he'd be gone anyway.

But that thought landed heavy in his chest. Who was he kidding? He didn't want to be on the move. He wanted to be here—with her.

And he had no idea what to do about it except keep showing up.

Chapter 1

Cali Jacobs knew the Cat Distribution System was at it again when her phone lit up with a string of texts.

Alert! Kitten spotted at trash bins outside the convenience store. Cute. Fast. Couldn't catch it. Let's keep our eyes open, team.

Saw it prancing down the sidewalk outside the cafe this morning. Gotta be a Maine Coon with that fluffy tail. If they hadn't just brought out my pancakes, I would've caught it.

Promises, Lynne. Promises.

More like priorities, Minka. They were YOUR pancakes. No more tips for you.

Guys! I saw it, too. Post office around noon, chasing a squirrel across the street. Kitty gets around! Anyone notice if it has a collar or tag?

She couldn't help but smile. Her plan to rescue all the cats in Autumn Ridge was already working.

Let's strategize at Nine Lives Club tonight, she texted back. *Mission: Maine Coon.*

Thumbs up emojis flooded her screen.

Cali pushed her horn-rimmed glasses up the bridge of her nose, inhaled the sweet, familiar smells of aged paper and binding glue, and got back to work on the staff's front desk schedule for the next two weeks.

CHAPTER 1

Being a librarian in Autumn Ridge was a far cry from corporate life in Eastmoor, her old metropolis several hours away by train. Eastmoor was gritty and cold New England, even in summer, with an industrial rail-and-factory backbone. Here it was inviting and warm somehow despite the cold and full of the fluffiest, cutest creatures she'd ever laid eyes on. More than once her eyes had misted over in the park and she found herself saying, "Aww. Would you look at that bunny or chipmunk or, well, anything worthy of a soft, uncontrollable squeal?" Every once in a while the residents made that warm feeling bubble to the surface, too.

But the cats dominated. Even though she'd only been in Autumn Ridge a couple of years, she'd noticed the uncanny number of stray cats who called the small town home. Cats outside the diner, pawing for crumbs. Cats with legs stretched above their heads in grooming outside the yoga studio. Cats curled in sleep against the library doors when she arrived each morning. She found herself arriving earlier and earlier to coax them to the back with bowls of milk and kibble. She'd scratch their heads and the sweet spot where their tails met their back then run back inside to intercept the staff. She never knew where they disappeared to when she peeked her head outside again, but she knew somewhere, somehow, some other Autumn Ridge citizen was preparing their lunch and waiting for them. Everyone had to chip in to make it work.

It wasn't fair, she thought, all those stray cats. But it made sense for a small, friendly town surrounded by miles of farmland. Strangers from the nearby city probably abandoned cats in the fields all the time, thinking they'd be better off fending for themselves than left at a shelter. But a shelter was exactly what Autumn Ridge needed and didn't have.

Enter the book club.

Before Cali arrived, the library held Saturday read-alouds for the kids, computer skills for retirees midweek, book fairs and puzzle-offs. Those fit easily into the tempo of the sleepy northeastern town. Then, at Cali's suggestion, the library held extended hours on Thursdays for an adults-only book club. Naturally, Cali was the host.

She wasn't too sure about the group at first. An uppity retiree, a sarcastic café owner, the florist, a hunky firefighter and a handful of other personalities. Their years of residence in the town alone outnumbered her years on earth by ten-fold, she was sure. So the stereotype of small towns breeding small minds was about to be tested. But the book club proved her wrong and quickly became *her people*—misfits with random interests and strong opinions. She remembered their first argument over whether the covers of Laurie Gilmore's Dream Harbor series were too innocent-looking for their heat levels.

"My young grandson found The *Cinnamon Bun Book Store* and asked if he could read it with us. It's because those covers all look like cartoons!" Mrs. Ellery insisted. "He even tried sneaking it into his school bag. Can you imagine what would've happened if he got to that beach scene in chapter 11?"

"Just buy him the coloring book," Bastet suggested. "Completely G-rated, if I'm not mistaken."

Over the next year they dove into banned books and queer romances, books about religious cults and the cult of consumerism together. Until one Thursday Cali woke up and realized she was home. Uprooting her city life to take a chance on Autumn Ridge had been the best thing to ever happen to her.

When book club conversation went off-topic one night—as it often did—the members discovered they'd all taken in one or more of the stray cats of Autumn Ridge. All of them, that is, except Cali. She'd wanted another cat ever since she inherited her grandmother's A-frame house overlooking the lake. But her heart was still broken over the loss of her first and only cat. A petite tabby with delicate paws and the greenest eyes she'd ever seen. They'd been together since she was a teenager. She missed kitty cuddles under her blanket each morning and the gentle meows reminding her it was time to be fed.

How was it that Autumn Ridge felt so right, but being in Autumn Ridge without a cat felt so wrong?

Cali never confessed this to anyone before. But as the book club members went round-robin, sharing stories of their own rescue kitties, she felt compelled. Every morning she set a can of pate on her back porch, wishing another stray would find her. It had attracted the attention of a few raccoons but not much else. She was a firm believer that the next cat finds *you*, not the other way around. It had been that way with her first.

The book club members rallied around her. Then a light bulb went off in Cali's head. Since Autumn Ridge couldn't afford to build a shelter, what if they—the book club members—made a network to rescue every stray cat that found its way to Autumn Ridge instead? Like a neighborhood watch, but without the crime or drama? Or like a group of matchmakers for cats?

"That may be the best idea I've ever heard, Cali," Mrs. Ellery said. "Count me in!"

Thus, the Nine Lives Club was born. They still loved their book club talks and debates, of course. But once the spines were closed, the discussion turned to the town's stray cats.

A thud sounded behind Cali, and she glanced over her shoulder, scanning the library. "Oops." An elderly volunteer sighed over a toppled cart of books while a kind patron whisked over to help her collect and reorganize them.

At least she'd whispered. That's more than could be said for the rest of the library this week. City Hall across the parking lot was adding the new courthouse building for almost six months. And although they were notified of possible noise before it began, no one was quite ready for the cacophony of jackhammers, grinders, and nail guns that suddenly appeared that week.

Cali nibbled at the temple of her rectangular glasses and turned her gaze toward a small mirror on her desk. Behind her, a dust storm from the construction swirled against the window. Even her view of the apple orchard in the distance was ruined by this renovation.

She sighed and pulled a hand through her wavy dark brown bob. A shock of white hair fell onto her forehead—a gift from the stress of Eastmoor. People always assumed she was older than she really was because of it. She puckered her lips and blew it away then checked her teeth for red lipstick stains. Four smiling brooches sparkled against her chest just beneath the Peter Pan collar of her khaki button-up blouse.

The screech of metal against metal made her jump from her seat. "Yikes. The only thing louder than the town's stray cats is this racket."

It was almost her turn at the help desk, so she shuffled out and over. She scribbled the last couple of names into time slots and grabbed her Purride & Purrjudice mug.

The hours ticked by, marked by an occasional bright scream or hiss from the construction outside. All the while a mid-pitched drill droned on, to the point she almost abandoned the desk. She tallied the usual bits to share with the staff:

CHAPTER 1

1. How many times have you been asked how to reset a password? Fourteen—which may have broken their current record. She'd have to check.
2. What was the most unique encounter you had today? An older man asked some very sensitive and specific questions about his odds for prostate cancer, to which Cali confessed she didn't know the answers. He huffed and patronizingly asked, "Didn't you have to read all the books to get hired at this library?" She recommended he speak with his doctor.

The hacking and sawing finally ceased at 5 p.m.. Relieved, Cali trekked back to her office to grab her blue trench coat and her wallet.

She only ever had time for a quick trip to Minka's café across the street before she needed to set up for the Nine Lives Club. Good thing Minka was also a member of the Nine Lives Club and would have her usual already waiting to get her through the night: a chicken salad sandwich in a buttery croissant, a warm coffee, and a treat for later. That's why she needed to run over to the café, to pick her treat. Since the weather chilled ever so slightly this morning, her mouth ached for pumpkin cream cheese muffins or those apple cider donuts the café carried around this time last year.

Then out of the corner of her eye she saw a swift, darting motion. Between the front steps of the library and the courthouse construction was the marbled gray fluffball the club had been texting about. Velvety black paws with faint tabby markings. It spotted her, too, and crouched down, frozen. Its eyes were a light gray, and its ears were big. Much too big for its tiny striped head and body—with pointed black tufts just above the soft pink inner ear.

She froze, too, but lowered to a crouch and raised her palms to signal harmlessness. "Here, kitty," she whispered in her slow-paced, high-pitched cat voice. "It's okay, baby. Psst psst psst. Aww. You're so cute."

It tilted its head but stayed vigilant. She suddenly wished she had a can of pate with her. Even something from the café might be enough to persuade it to come closer. It looked a little thin beneath all that long fur. Her heart leapt into her throat.

Then she noticed another thing that made her heart do tricks. One of the construction workers appeared from the parking lot between the library and City Hall. A man, shirtless and muscular, with a dark tattoo sleeve wrapped around one of his thick forearms. He paused when he spotted her, his cheeks flushed from working all day. From underneath his construction hat peered two steely gray eyes. Freckles peppered the bridge of his nose and cheekbones and faded toward a wide jaw that framed his plump, ruddy lips.

She watched the Adam's apple bob in his throat, his jaw clenched and his eyes flicked back toward the stray.

Cali knew exactly what he wanted.

"Psst," she hissed. "Back off. I don't need any help. You're going to scare it away."

He wiped sweat off his brow with his gloves and inched closer to the kitten. Big hands, she noticed. But his eyes steeled against her instructions. He stepped closer. There couldn't have been more than 10 feet between each of them and the kitten. Cali could feel the tension surge between them.

"I wasn't trying to help. But *you're* going to scare him away if *you* make that silly noise one more time." His voice was low and rumbling. It made Cali's belly warm.

CHAPTER 1

"Shh." She crept closer, keeping her movements small. The construction worker mirrored her on his side of the cat. She wanted to throw something at him but knew how careful they'd need to be to pull this off. She didn't trust him. "And just what makes you think it's a boy?"

"Just look at it. It's clearly a boy." He let out a sigh. "And I see what you're doing over there. Stop. It's going to bolt off."

The Maine Coon adjusted its stance so it could eye them both. Its whiskers wiggled.

Good, kitty. Don't run now, her mind pleaded. If she could just get close enough to reach.

"We'll just see who it chooses, okay?" Cali whispered, practically on her knees. Construction dude be damned. She ran track in high school. So she could outrun Mr. Muscles if that cat would just let her get another foot closer.

She reached out until she had one hand above its back and another near its stomach. She could hear the nervous purr growing loud as her hands closed around it. Then it bolted out of her arms and across the street. When she glanced down at her wrist, she saw blood. The sting was intense. Both Cali and the construction worker watched in dismay as the kitten's fluffy tail disappeared behind the café.

"Dammit," they said in unison.

Cali stood and crossed her arms over her chest. The scratch on her wrist stung like hell. When the construction worker approached, tall and flexing, she thought she caught a sympathetic glint in his eyes. Impossible. She wasn't going to let some brute intimidate her. The Eastmoor girl in her rallied.

"What you do that for?" she seethed.

"Me? I warned you not to creep up on him. He ran away, just like I said he would." The tendons in his jawline flexed.

"Someone here clearly doesn't know anything about cats."

Now that was crossing a line. "I've had cats—well, a cat, singular—most of my life, I'll have you know!"

"Well it didn't look or sound like it, the way you approach him."

"Ugh, stop calling it a him. You can't tell just by looking at it! And cats are drawn to soft, high-pitched sounds, especially the 'psst psst psst' one that apparently pissed you off. If someone here doesn't know anything about cats, that someone is you."

She pressed an index finger into his pecs and immediately regretted it. His flesh didn't give against her touch. But she caught a whiff of sweat and his cologne and something woodsy all around them that made her lightheaded and tingly. She licked her lips.

He glanced down the street in the direction of the cat then back at her. "Wow," he said, exhaling through his nose, long and slow. "You're unbelievable. You know that?"

"Well, you're ... you're ..." *Stop drowning in those eyes and speak, Cali.* "Arrogant," she muttered back. It was all she could think to say.

One corner of his mouth curled up. She lowered her hand, and he turned and strutted away to City Hall. Cali felt blood creeping up her neck and into her ears as she watched his jeans, hung just right. The deep V of muscles that made his long torso. On his right shoulder was another tattoo—or half of one. It was hard to see this far away, but Cali thought she could make out the black curve of a cat's tail, enveloping his wing bone.

When he reached the end of the sidewalk, he turned around again. He pulled a tape measure from his back pocket, slid it out, and lifted it between them, as if sizing her up.

"Caught you staring," he yelled.

CHAPTER 1

Cali frowned then, with one final huff of hatred, dashed across the street toward the café. This time, her cheeks were the ones flushed.

Chapter 2

Cali slammed the café door so hard the bell above her nearly rang off the mounting.

Minka had been wiping down tables, but she stopped and stared wide-eyed at Cali.

"You're not going to believe what just happened, Minka!" The smell of warm, sugary pastries and brewed coffee did nothing to assuage Cali's anger.

Minka squinted at Cali through perfectly drawn cat-eye eyeliner. "Uhh ... the library board finally heard you out on the banned books display?"

"No, I wish. It's on the agenda for the board meeting this month, though. My last chance before Banned Books Week."

"Okay, so ... you won the lottery?"

"Does this look like the face of a woman who won the lottery?" The volume of Cali's voice surprised even her. Frustrated-librarian-hiding-in-car level of loud. She plopped into one of the café chairs and watched as her glasses slid down her nose and onto the floor. She threw up her hands. "August is out to get me, Minka."

Minka clutched her towel to her chest. "Cali—you're bleeding. Don't move."

Cali followed Minka's gaze to her wrist, peeking from underneath a blood-speckled trench coat sleeve and groaned. "Vintage," she muttered. "My grandmother's. I just found it in the basement last week!"

The corner of Minka's mouth twitched. Her telltale sign of incoming sarcasm. "Okay, Charlie Sheen. It's not tiger's blood. All it requires is a little stain remover. On the other hand is your carved and leaking flesh. Just don't ... move."

Minka disappeared into the kitchen as Cali waited. When Minka returned, she was carrying Cali's to-go bag, a bottle of rubbing alcohol, cotton balls, and a hot, wet towel. Cali watched her friend wash the wound and sucked air between her teeth as Minka pressed the alcohol into her skin. They could both make out the puffy scratches rising from her flesh like bad seams. At least the alcohol stopped the bleeding.

"Better get a bandage on that soon," said Minka. "Or a wrap. I'm out."

Cali sighed. "I've got some bandages at my desk back at the library."

Minka's tuxedo cat jumped onto the table between them and nuzzled into Cali's shoulder, vibrating with affection.

"Aww, thanks, Purrcy." Cali scratched his head then rubbed at her wrist, which itched like crazy now. She turned to Minka. "So, as you might've guessed, I found that Maine Coon."

Minka's eyes widened. "And our tiniest, fuzziest foster did this to you? Maybe it's not the sweet kitten as we all assumed."

"No, I'm sure it is," Cali insisted. "It was just the circumstances. I saw it outside the library on my walk over here. But so did this other guy—one of the construction workers getting off work at the same time. The kitten would've been mine if he'd just minded his own damn business."

Minka's expression changed to worry as she resumed cleaning the café. "You think he was trying to hurt it? Or shoo it off the construction site?"

"No, he was trying to help me."

Minka's brows creased together. "How very ..." she considered Cali's face, "dare he?"

"Right?!"

Minka stared across from her at the tiny round table. "Okay, girl. Either I'm confused or we're in the middle of a *Vanderpump Rules* episode and this 'isn't about the pasta' at all."

Cali's nose scrunched up. "I have no idea what you're talking about."

Purrcy meowed repeatedly at Cali. "Thanks, Purrs. Everyone needs a Vander-splainer in their lives. I'll take it from here." She ushered the cat off the table and wiped away the paw prints. "What I mean is: Why are you mad at some secret undercover agent sent to help end Mission: Maine Coon before it ever really got started? Isn't that a good thing?"

"Not when it ends in this." Cali raised her wrist.

"Nah, kitty just got spooked. It happens with strays. And if I'm being honest, you sound spooked, too, Cals. This is bigger than a scratch. What's up?"

Cali felt a lump in her throat. "He ... he wanted to keep the cat."

"Oh." Minka's expression softened, and she reached across the table to place one hand lightly over Cali's.

This meant she understood. She understood perfectly that Cali's dreams of having another cat "find" her were not only dashed moments ago but dashed in an epic way. Minka was like that sometimes—full of wit and pop culture references until it was the heart's turn to speak. Then she'd get all quiet and just let things, well, be. It was one of the many qualities

Cali appreciated about her. That and Minka remembered her neurotic coffee order after the first visit to the café: *Can I get a triple-shot oat milk latte, half-decaf, extra hot but not scalding, with one pump vanilla and one and a half pumps hazelnut. But could you do half-sweet on the hazelnut?*

Now Minka just called it the Oat Couture.

"Well, you just point me in the direction of this jerk. Next time I see him, it's hot coffee in the eyeball for him." She was teasing, but it made Cali smile. Then Cali remembered the construction worker's pressing gaze and felt her cheeks flood with warmth. "There's my girl." Minka rose from the table and continued cleaning. "Seriously, though, was it that grumpy foreman? Always shouting demeaning curses at the crew unless he's got something in his mouth? Potbelly in front, more cracks than a crème brûlée in back?"

"No, it was one of the younger guys. Um. Tall, tattoos, umm ... " Cali licked her lips as she remembered the perspiration trickling down his chiseled abs and into the band of his jeans. What was the phrase she was looking for? Rugged? Sharp-featured? Unnervingly attractive? "Athletic."

Minka blinked twice and scurried back over to the table with a squeal. The sound almost startled Cali out of her chair. "Ethan Cross?" Minka said with heavy, breathless emphasis on each word. "Ethan wanted your rescue cat? You are the luckiest woman in all of Autumn Ridge, Cali!"

"How do you know his name?" Cali asked skeptically.

"Because I'm certifiable. No, he comes in here to get his thermos filled every morning before work. We've met. We talk. Did you know he's already got a cat? I'm surprised you two haven't run into each other already, all things considered."

"What do you mean by that?" Cali narrowed her eyes.

"Well, he's always got a book in his hands. Each morning, he takes the outside table and chair—you know, the one that faces the library?—and he reads his book until half the thermos is gone. Then he comes back in for a top-off, pays, and leaves."

Cali's head was spinning. "No, that can't be. I – I enter through the front door every day and I've never seen a guy sitting at that table outside."

Minka shook her head slowly, her expression filled with disappointment. "My dear friend, that is because you are blind."

"Come on."

"No, I mean it. Have you *seen* that crew working on the new courthouse for the past six months?"

Cali softened her voice. "Not really. I was focused on work ... and the banned books effort and feeding the strays."

"All wonderful distractions. Commendable, really." Minka exhaled a low, deep breath. "Cali, there may be a few crew with tattoos, but there's only one guy who someone could objectively call 'athletic'. I've seen him with my own two eyes."

"So you know how rude he is then."

"He's been nothing but nice to me." Minka smirked.

Salt in the wound, and Cali felt a little stung. She tried not to show it, but she was a little jealous.

"That's because you hold the nectar of life—a.k.a. coffee—in your hands, Minka. We're all at your mercy. I, on the other hand, was trying to go after a cat that he apparently also wanted." *Badly.*

Minka grabbed a napkin and fanned herself. "That means you haven't even seen him without his construction hat then, have you? Hair for days. The kind you could run your fingers through. A young Cillian Murphy circa *Red Eye*, girl."

"A little compassion here? This man is my cat nemesis. He's testing the whole premise of the Cat Distribution System. Finders keepers. I spotted it first."

Minka shrugged. "Well, Cillian's the villain in most of his movies, too."

"Minka!"

"What? You've never fallen for the villain?"

Cali considered for a fleeting second then shook her head. "That's not the point. When he left, he pulled out his —"

"Ohh!" squealed Minka.

Cali rolled her eyes. "Tape measure and acted like he was sizing me up. Can you believe that?"

Minka gestured toward the clock on the wall then at the dessert display. "Please. Pick your dessert and get going already. You promised booze at book club tonight, and I need this after the week I've had."

"Wine," Cali corrected. "I promised wine. We're not allowed to have hard liquor at library events."

"Whatever. You know I spike my coffee before I bring it over for book club anyway, right?"

"Explains the cheerfulness."

"Hello?" Minka huffed. "I'm always cheerful."

Cali grabbed her to-go bag and cup. "Apple cider donut?"

"None just yet. But soon. Or so my shipper promises. How about a slice of peach pie? Last chance before the fall flavors arrive."

"You know what?" Cali frowned. "I'll just skip it tonight. Kind of lost my appetite anyway."

Minka offered a sympathetic glance as Cali headed out the door. "That Maine Coon will show up again, Cali, or The Nine will find it. Promise."

A small glimmer of hope rekindled in Cali's chest as she made her way back across the street toward the library. The sun was setting earlier these days. The skyline darkened from crimson and lavender to a deep blue and an ever-so-soft chill kissed her bare cheeks.

The library greeted her with its quiet, and she dimmed the lights. All they had were children's bandages in the first aid kit, but it didn't matter to her if there were blue monsters or tiny kittens latched onto her skin. What mattered was that the scratch stopped stinging. She applied ointment, which brought some relief, then several bandages. She soaked the trench coat sleeve under the sink in the bathroom then flung it on the back of her office chair to dry.

Nearly 7 p.m. The brown bag dinner from the café sat untouched on her desk in her office, and she didn't know when or if she'd get around to eating it. But the warmth of the Oat Couture warmed her hands and filled her belly with calm. She savored the last sips as she did a cross-check of the room. Clear plastic cups sat on a round table in the center of the chairs she'd rearranged into a circle. One uncorked bottle of pinot grigio, a bottle of merlot, and her tattered, multi-bookmarked, personal copy of *They Both Die at the End* by Adam Silvera rested between them. Although it was young adult—and a bit of a risk to pose it to an adult book club—Cali hoped the other themes would strike chords across the club's team members, young and old.

She'd never confessed this, but she still sometimes felt butterflies before a library event. Guiding people through a candid and sometimes emotional conversation about fiction wasn't like project management. The learning curve she'd experienced after she earned her degree was immense. But she was getting better at throwing an idea out there and not expecting others to follow her.

A knock sounded at the library door. Leo gave her a nod from outside, his dimple casting a shadow against his cheek. Cali had to admit, when she'd first moved to Autumn Ridge, that dimple almost did her in. But he only saw her as a friend. It was clear he had eyes for someone else.

Mrs. Ellery waved her gloved hand, and Cali rushed toward them, holding the door open as the remaining members spilled in.

When Lynne, the owner of the only bar in Autumn Ridge, spotted the alcohol, she started pouring. "White for you, Tabitha?" Lynne filled the small, clear cup to the brim.

"Oh no. If Lynne's pouring, we're all in trouble," Tabitha cautioned. "Someone please disarm her."

"Nonsense. Just because you ended up dancing on the bar once doesn't mean that's everyone's fate." She turned. "White for you, too, Mrs. Ellery?"

"I actually prefer the merlot—but only a bit. Otherwise it'll be shenanigans from 7:30 onward."

Everyone's eyes widened. Cali blinked from behind her glasses.

"Noted!" Leo teased. "Hide the tables from this one, too, Cali. Didn't know you were such a party animal, Mrs. Ellery."

She grinned, lowering her eyes, and shook her perfectly coiffed gray hair. "You wish, Leo."

They all burst into laughter.

"I'll have some of whatever she's having!" said Minka.

"You look like a red, Cali. May I?" Lynne grabbed Cali's Purride and Purrjudice mug and served her a decent amount. "Now, onto this—"

Another knock echoed from the front of the library. Cali

squinted but couldn't make out a face. She glanced around the room, noting everyone was already here. "Just a moment," she said, standing. "I'll be right back."

"I'll come with you," Leo offered.

She smoothed out the pleats of her A-line skirt and adjusted her glasses. "Please. Enjoy your wine. I'm sure it's nothing." But her heart beat in her throat, and her hands tightened into fists as she shuffled toward the doors.

Back at the Eastmoor library, they'd given all the librarians self-defense "boot camp" training. Granted, it was the same training the seniors received—in fact, the seniors were in the class with them. But Cali had a few tricks up her sleeve should anyone try to mess with her.

But when she reached the door, she felt her breath hitch in her rib cage. Two dreamy blue-gray eyes beamed at her from behind the glass.

She opened the door but couldn't move. "Ethan?" she whispered. "What are you doing here?"

He towered over her, dressed in black jeans and a gray, rib-knit Henley that hugged his physique. His dark hair was softly disheveled, parted loosely at the temple with waves brushing forward and framing his brow. The gray of his shirt nearly matched his eyes.

"And how do you know my name, cat thief?" A smirk stretched across his lips, the kind of grin that belonged to someone who never lost a bet.

Cali flinched. "I'm not—I didn't mean—" She found herself tongue-tied. "It was Minka," she confessed.

"I'm impressed with how fast you do your research."

He stepped closer and leaned against the doorframe. So close he could press into her if he took just one step more. So close she could make out a shadow of stubble along his jawbone. So close she could smell his cologne, like cedarwood and vanilla with spice. She felt the grip in her hands loosen, a slow rush of heat building in her abdomen.

"Hey!" Leo hooted from the back of the library. "Look what the cat dragged in!"

Chapter 3

Ethan's gaze reluctantly pulled away from Cali's face as Leo ran up behind her. Side by side, they could've passed as brothers, minus the dimple thing. Both dark hair, well built. But Ethan had more of an edge to him.

"Glad to see you finally made it. C'mon in, man." Leo wedged between them, wrapped an arm around Ethan, and escorted him away. Cali made a mental note to murder Leo later and locked the door again. She could overhear Leo continue as he pulled up an extra seat for Ethan. The circle widened to make room for them. "I said Nine Lives doesn't start until about 8. What brings you here early, buddy?"

Cali cleared her throat and took her seat again at the opposite side of the circle. She sent an icy stare in Ethan's direction.

"Well ..." Ethan started, hesitantly, piecing together how he may have interrupted something sacred. "I was going to grab a bite at the café, but it was closed." He glanced over at Minka, and she waved like a schoolgirl. "Then I thought I'd just grab a beer and wait instead, but the bar was also closed." His eyes flicked between Lynne and the wine bottles. "So when I saw the light on inside the library, I figured I'd knock." He glanced around the entire group once more. "Did I interrupt something? Why do I feel like I maybe should've known the secret handshake to be let in?" His eyes landed back on Cali, and she shifted in her seat.

"Oh no," Tabitha chimed in. "We're just the book club. And the Nine Lives club. Same thing. We were about to dive into *They Both Die at the End*. You read it?"

"Of course."

Of course? What did he mean 'of course'?

He leaned forward in his chair and rested his elbows on his knees when someone passed him a cup of wine. Cali watched as he pushed the Henley sleeves up to his elbows, revealing the tattoos. "Sorry," he said with a muffled snicker, "I don't think I caught everyone's names." He stared across at Cali. "Let's start with you."

Cali felt her face light on fire. Her hand instinctively rose to her collar, and she found her fingers fumbling the buttons along her chest. "Oh, me? I'm Cali." She cleared her throat again. "Cali Jacobs. I'm the librarian here."

"And the one who started the book club," added Minka.

"And the Nine Lives club," said Leo. "She's being modest."

"I don't think we've ever seen you modest before, darling," Mrs. Ellery said with a wink.

Cali ran her fingers through her curls. "So, um, Ethan ... " She really did like the way his name sounded, the way her tongue pressed against her teeth when she said it. "Who else don't you know here? We should probably start soon."

Ethan turned toward the florist, Freya, and a couple others, including Mrs. Ellery. Once the conversation died down, Cali interjected. "Since this was my pick, I'll start with the elephant in the room: the title. Were you surprised by the ending?"

A heated debate immediately ensued. Ethan rolled his eyes when Cali romanticized Mateo's passive nature, and she returned the gesture when his speech about life's randomness started to sound more like a lecture than a discussion. She accused him of being "too practical" in his takes. He called her "too soft" for needing a happy-ever-after. But then they both brought up the subtle-yet-possible direct involvement of Death-Cast in the main characters' downfalls, which left the rest of the book club speechless. If Cali wasn't mistaken, she caught the barest ghost of a grin on Ethan's face—a true and genuine smile, not a smirk.

"Is this one of the banned books you're trying to get in the display, Cali?" Freya asked.

Cali nodded. "If it's LGBTQ+, you can bet someone doesn't want you reading it. In fact, if it's got sex, race, religion, or anything not strictly 'vanilla,' it's inevitably challenged. That's why I wish the library board would hear me out. Books like this need more attention."

"They're just stick-in-the-muds, Cali," Mrs. Ellery offered. "I should know. I grew up with most of them. It's not that we shouldn't have a banned book display. It's merely that the library's never had one before."

Leo downed what was left of his wine. "Not to break topic, but we're already well past 8 p.m. Tell us more about this Maine Coon you spotted, Ethan. We've been texting about it all day."

Leo's pivot jarred no one, it seemed, but Cali, who shifted uncomfortably in her seat as Ethan recited the history between him and the Maine Coon kitten—and its stray mother before it ever appeared. He'd clearly found it before Cali had. A wave of embarrassment crept over her.

"I think his mother died," Ethan explained. "I got all the construction crew guys looking out for his mom. We almost got her into a trap so I could get her spayed and checked out and bring her home. The Great Catsby's been wanting a brother or sister," he confessed. Cali almost spit out her wine. *Catsby!* Ethan saw her hand fly to her face but pretended not to notice. "Then she disappeared," he continued, "and this little guy shows up on site instead, same colors, same tree where she always waited and watched for the lady who put kibble out behind the library every morning."

His voice trailed off. Cali was so flustered she could sink into her chair. No, through it. Right through the carpet and into the core of the Earth. No one knew she'd been doing that. No one needed to know! That was between her and the cats.

In a long, comedic delay, Minka exclaimed, "Oh! That must've been Cali you saw!"

"Stay with the class, dear," Mrs. Ellery quipped. "Now back to the plot." She gestured for Ethan to go on.

"He's too young to be running out here alone, especially around a work site. I'm just worried about him. So when Leo here told me there was, like, a cat rescue group thing in town, I said I'd swing by."

Cali couldn't help flinching every time Ethan referred to the kitten as "him."

"Oh, don't let me forget to add you to the text thread, man," said Leo. "We'll find your cat."

Everyone but Minka nodded their heads in agreement. Minka glanced over at Cali, who was silently fuming. How easily she'd been out-voted as the Maine Coon's chosen rescuer. Yes, Ethan had a history with the cat—and its mom if his assumptions were correct. But Cali was the one sacrificing kibble and pâté every day and kick-starting the Nine Lives Club and laying all the groundwork. More than simply "keeping an eye out" for the cat. That had to count for something.

"And then Cali and I both saw him outside the library today."

"You did? Did you two catch it?" Freya asked them.

Cali's icy stare threatened to bore a hole in Ethan's skull. "No. It ran off."

"Because—"

"So what's the plan?" Minka interrupted them.

Bless you, Minka. Cali sighed.

"Well, if it's smart, it'll stay away from the construction noise," said Lynne. "Not sure you two will find it around here again."

Cali *had* noticed a slight attendance drop in the morning's stray cat kibble line when she opened the library this past week.

"But if Cali's leaving food out behind the library, maybe they will," suggested Freya.

"Honestly, with as many places as we observed that kitten today, it could turn up anywhere. We just all need to be ready when any of us finds it again." Leave it to Mrs. Ellery to offer wisdom and some direction.

"But what does 'ready' mean?"

"I've got an idea." Cali jumped from her seat and shuffled back to her office. The crinkled, half-empty bag of cat food was tucked into one of her desk drawers. She set her mug on top of the desk and grabbed the kibble, plus several brown bags she always kept on hand for craft days or just-in-case moments. Once, when a young woman came to the front desk in tears, she'd even used one of those bags to discreetly pass her some pads.

She rejoined the group and started scooping small amounts of the kibble into each of the bags. "If we agree to keep one of these with us at all times, our odds increase." She passed around the bags and a permanent marker so they could each write their names on the outside. "It's not foolproof. From what Ethan and I saw today, it gets spooked easily. But it's bound to get hungry enough soon with all that scurrying around town."

Next thing she knew, Ethan was raising his hand. "Um, I think I got the wrong bag."

"Why's that?" she scoffed.

"This one's got a, uh, sandwich. Smells like chicken salad." He raised his eyebrows and that stupid lip started to curl again. "I mean, he *may* want this, but I'll probably eat it before he has a chance."

"Shoot. That was my dinner. Sorry." She distracted herself with more kibble and bags. But when he tried passing it back, Cali shook her head at him. "You want it? Minka made it, so it's obviously amazing."

"But it's yours."

"Well, I'm not hungry anymore." *And feeling a little buzzed*, she had to admit. *Why do I always get so friendly after a few sips of wine?* "You said you didn't get dinner yet. So might as well."

He shrugged, and she shrugged back at him. Then he devoured the sandwich in three bites. "Mmm. That *is* good, Minka," he said, mouth still half-full of food. "Nice work."

Cali and Minka exchanged a glance, and Minka chortled into her sleeve.

Between the cats and this guy, Cali, you're up for sainthood.

She shoved the last cat food bag into his hands and started returning chairs to their desks. The Nine—technically ten now, she realized—paired off, whispering goodbyes or chuckling as they made their way to the library exit. Cali assumed Ethan and Leo would be absorbed in conversation, but within a matter of moments Ethan was hovering over her shoulder again. One sweet and spicy whiff of his cologne gave him away.

"I can help," he offered, a chairback already gripped in one of his strong hands.

Cali felt her mouth go dry. "Over there," she gestured, toward the desk as far away from her as possible.

Two by two they replaced the chairs between them until they stood face to face again.

"Walk you to your car?" he asked. "Just want to make sure you make it home okay."

Cali laughed uncomfortably and pulled a curl behind her ear. "I—I'll be fine. I feel lucky to say this, but Autumn Ridge isn't exactly an unsafe town."

His nose crinkled. "But you locked the library doors before book club."

"Oh." She had to think for a moment. "Habit. I used to work in Eastmoor."

"That explains a lot."

Cali eyed him, not sure if that was a knowing stare or another tease. He held her gaze, refusing to give her any more clarity. She felt faint just looking at him, his pecs and mouth and fragrant hair dangerously close. Close enough to touch. She could hardly breathe. "But aren't—aren't you and Leo going to catch up or something?"

"Nah, he's gotta feed his cat."

"If Fred didn't sneak out again," Cali snorted.

"Leo's cat's an escape artist?"

"Notoriously so." Cali nervously tucked a curl behind her ear. "Well, what about Catsby? Don't you have to get home to him?"

"Her and no. Catsby's probably sitting on the couch like a loaf, still digesting her dinner."

Her. Of course.

Cali gulped and nodded her head. "I guess I'll grab my purse from my office then. Meet me at the front doors."

Chapter 4

The dark, crisp, early autumn air was intoxicating. Not cool enough for Cali to see her breath yet but cool enough to justify leaving her windows open tonight as she slept. The faint buzz from the wine at book club was already wearing off, but in its place was a warm, cozy feeling in her belly. She clutched her trench with one hand and her purse with the other as she and Ethan walked down the long handicap ramp toward the parking lot.

"You're all smiles," Ethan noted. He'd pushed up his sleeves again, exposing the intricate tattoo that wrapped his left forearm down to the wrist, while he waited for her at the door.

"The wine helps," she quipped, "and fall is my favorite season."

He shrugged. "Fall's okay. I'm more of a winter guy myself."

She asked him why, and she expected some contrived response like "I hate the heat" or "I love snow." But what he said instead was "More time to cook."

"You do not!" she blurted and let out a startled laugh, mostly out of surprise. Maybe the wine wasn't wearing off after all. She regretted it the instant his face changed.

"I'm a really good cook!" he insisted.

Cali didn't know how to counter that one. "But can't—can't

CHAPTER 4

you cook in the summer, too?" she asked. "Spring? Fall?" *Three questions into twenty questions already. Way to go, Cali.*

He straightened sharply, his spine rigid, and stuck his hands in his pockets. "Winter means less daylight and, therefore, shorter days on the construction site. Fewer hours there means more time at home, perfecting my *coq au vin*."

Cali couldn't tell if he was serious or messing with her again. "So you hibernate in winter with wine and French stew? Very manly."

Ethan chuckled at the hazing as they strode toward the only car left in the library's parking lot. "This one's mine," she said.

Her Honda didn't exactly scream witty, early-thirties woman, but it was reliable and came with the house. Cali never drove in the city, but she was just glad she had a car here—and a short and mostly traffic-less ride each workday to boot. Autumn Ridge only had a handful of stoplights and a sprinkling of stop signs to navigate. If it weren't for the fact that her grandmother's A-frame house and the lake were on the outskirts of town, she could have still been fine without a vehicle.

She unlocked her car and turned toward Ethan, thinking she'd say thanks and speed off, take some time to wonder why she felt pulled to the warmth of his body the longer they'd walked side by side. But the way the moonlight illuminated his hair and face and chiseled torso, like one of those Roman sculptures, made her swallow her words.

"What are you doing right now?" Ethan asked, jarring her from her trance.

Was he about to ask her out for drinks? After they'd already had drinks? She knew herself well enough to know no good could come from this. And this man was transitory anyway. Here one construction project, gone for the next. To indulge in any thought of having something serious with him was naive.

"Washing my hair," she lied.

"Cali ..."

"No, really. Earlier today, because of the construction, I just walked into a big cloud of—" She flung her hands wide to illustrate, and her purse shot off her shoulder like a missile. The insides of the purse spilled across the asphalt several feet away from them. "Well, damn," she said, almost in disbelief.

"Remind me to duck next time," said Ethan.

He jogged toward her purse and crouched down, about to collect everything for her. But she ran up beside him, fearful of what he might find. Seven different shades of nearly identical red lipstick. Loose cat treats rattling around like Tic Tacs. That terrible half-blinking photo on her driver's license. A small vial labeled "tears of my enemies" that was really just filled with water but made her smile each time she saw it. It was all on display on the sidewalk for Ethan.

He casually scooped up the vial and read it as she tucked the rest back into the purse.

"You are full of surprises, Cali Jacobs," he said. But he made no moves to return it. She noted how he said her full name, the way it lingered on his lips.

If Cali was being honest, that vial was her most treasured possession since moving to Autumn Ridge. She and Minka had found it during a girls' trip to Salem, Massachusetts last fall. A reminder of Cali's first friendship here. The same vial was buried in Minka's purse somewhere, too.

She waited a few beats, until his lips curved upward into a restrained smile. "Careful," she warned him. "I've got room in there for your tears, too." His gaze softened, and the vial passed between their hands, their fingertips touching. Cali felt the warmth and electricity between them but tried to write it off as static. She cleared her throat and pressed her shoulders back. "What would we do?" she asked begrudgingly.

His eyebrows lifted. "'We'?"

"Right now. Hypothetically. If my shampoo schedule allowed it."

"Oh." The question seemed to startle him, and he ran thick fingers through his hair as he looked away. "I just thought maybe we could, uh, search for the cat."

Cali rolled her eyes. "In the dark?"

"Why not? Don't you think, between us, we'd find him quickly? Cats are most active at dawn and dusk anyway. He's bound to be around here somewhere."

"Ethan," she tsked. "It's well past dusk. And the last time that cat was *between us* it bolted and left a mark on me." She lifted her bandaged wrist to remind him. "I'll believe in midnight cat hunts when you show up here with *coq au vin*."

"Next Thursday then?"

"For book club?"

"No," he said. "After. *Coq au vin* and wandering around in the dark together."

She clicked her keys, the car chirping to life, and gave him a mock-sweet smile. "Careful, Ethan. That sounds dangerously close to a date."

Chapter 5

Cali arrived at the library the next morning refreshed. She couldn't remember the last time she'd been able to sleep with the windows open. April? May? However long ago it had been, it was too long.

She always felt different—better even—and slept deeper, too, whenever the weather chilled. The sunrise was lazy this morning, taking its time to pour through her bedroom window. The air felt thinner and crisp. The quiet hammer of woodpeckers, the comforting smell of wood smoke mingling with the cool air, the distant echo of marching bands practicing for the high school football games. Everything about Autumn Ridge looked brighter on her way into work, despite not snagging any cats with the pâté on the back porch again.

There was just something magical about the transition to autumn for Cali, because she could dig into the part of her wardrobe that celebrated the season. While she'd been noticed by many in Autumn Ridge for her vintage-inspired style ever since her arrival—red lips, horn-rimmed glasses, cardigans, blouses with bows, handmade circle skirts—her personality really shone through this morning. A circle skirt with a woodsy print of squirrels with acorns and fall foliage paired with a slim, emerald-green button-up, another cat brooch peeking out of

CHAPTER 5

the left breast pocket. This time it was a black cat with yellow eyes, one of her favorites. The only thing that would have made today sweeter, she reasoned, was if there'd been a cat curled beside her head on the pillow or buried in the covers or stretched across her belly on top of the quilt. A little pang of sadness beat in her chest, the feel and memory of her first and only cat resurfacing.

She journeyed up the handicap ramp toward the double doors of the library, kitten heels softly clicking against the concrete, when she remembered what Minka had said about Ethan. How he'd been sitting there, across the street, every morning, with a thermos of black coffee. And reading—or watching. Perhaps watching her.

That's ridiculous, Cali. He didn't even know your name until yesterday. Why would he—?

She couldn't help but glance over.

Ethan's stormy gray eyes locked with hers. He had a phone pressed to one ear and a cocky smile on his face, the warm steam from the thermos rising up to his lips.

Cali chided herself for never taking note of him there before. Had he been sitting out there every day for the past six months? Or just more recently? She knew now he'd been spying on her as she fed the strays behind the library each morning. But had he been spying on her when she showed up to the library, too?

Then she realized she'd stopped walking up the ramp.

Ethan noticed, too, and lifted his hand in a casual wave, as if to say *Caught you staring again.* She debated not waving back at all, pretending she was staring across the street at something else. Instead, she pretended to rummage through her purse for the library keys before granting him the world's smallest wave back.

Fortunately, he didn't stalk her while she fed the strays out back this morning. No Maine Coon kitten in sight either. The construction noises didn't kick-start until 9 a.m. But when they did, they drowned out the lovely orchestra of autumn noises that had accompanied Cali that morning. Since it was Friday, the library was slammed, and she found herself swamped handling overdue notices, checking the book drops and sorting returned materials, and answering patron questions as everyone rushed to grab their books, DVDs, and puzzles for the weekend.

She retreated to her office to catch her breath, only to find herself breathless again when she glanced out her office window to find Ethan, shirtless again, in her purview. It was all she could do to peel her eyes from veins running like cords down his forearms, the play of shadow and light along his sharply cut obliques. She shut the window blind before he could catch her and got back to work.

All through her workday, the Nine Lives Club was messaging. The Maine Coon kitten was seen begging for scraps near the park's picnic benches, chasing mice in the dusty back lot of Bastet's auto repair shop, even perched on a tombstone at the cemetery. But no one was able to catch it.

Between the Friday patrons and text message pings, Cali was exhausted by closing time and filled with a wistful hunger for the chicken salad sandwich she'd given to Ethan the previous night. So as soon as the clock struck 6 p.m., she grabbed her purse and trench and bee-lined for Minka's café.

The September skyline was waiting there for her, with flocks of geese printing dark chevrons across the fading blue. She noticed the first reds and burnt oranges at the crown of the maples, shifting in the wind. The sun was dipping faster these days, an amber coin sliding into a pocket behind the faraway hills.

She took a moment on the library steps to breathe in the faint apple-sweetness when she saw him again. Ethan. Fully clothed in a faded gray t-shirt this time but walking toward the café several yards from her nonetheless. Her stomach clenched momentarily, and she had to remind herself she was headed there for food, not him. But her pulse ticked up when his shadow fell in step beside hers.

"Hey."

His voice was so soft and disarming, she almost wondered if he'd had a bad day.

"Oh. Hey, Ethan." She pretended she hadn't noticed him leaving the construction site at—coincidentally—the same time she left the library.

"Any word on the cat?"

"Lots, actually. The Nine have been reporting on its whereabouts all day long, but no one's caught it yet."

They both paused in front of the café door. Cali expected him to smell gross after a long day of work, but an irresistible scent washed over her. Spiced, with a hint of skin-hugging sweetness.

He grasped the handle of the café door and opened it for her. "Ladies first."

His height made the door look smaller, as though he belonged to a world a little bigger than everyone else's. There was a steadiness in the way he stood, the way he moved—grounded and unhurried, like the earth tilted to accommodate him.

Cali raised an eyebrow in surprise then slipped past him and into the café.

"Any seat!" Minka yelled from the back of the café, unaware

it was the two of them. But when she peeked through the window to the kitchen, her eyes lit up at the sight of them side by side. She mouthed *Oh my God!* at Cali through the narrow kitchen window as Ethan scanned the room for a table.

"Evening, Ethan," someone called from the corner booth. Another turned and waved from the counter.

Cali blinked. Half the café seemed to know him. Since when did construction workers collect fan clubs? Then she remembered the way he'd looked without his shirt on yesterday. She could think of a few reasons.

Cali found her mouth suddenly dry. "I was just going to grab something to go," she tried to tell Ethan, not really wanting to linger. But when she glanced over, Ethan was already planted in the cozy booth next to her, gesturing as if he expected her to sit across from him.

Cali frowned.

"This booth not to your liking? We can move anywhere you'd like." He gestured around the café. "Please, I owe you for that croissant you donated to the Hungry Ethan Fund last night at Nine Lives."

She offered him a faint smile. "It's just that I—"

"Need to wash your hair?" he quipped. A glimmer of knowing passed between them. "C'mon. Sit. I want to know where they've seen that cat today anyway. He hasn't been near City Hall at all. I looked."

Before Cali could answer, Minka swept up to the booth, setting down an empty mug and a fresh pot of coffee in front of Ethan and a steaming cup of Oat Couture in front of Cali.

"Chicken salad croissant and two apple cider donuts for Cali, coming right up," she said brightly. "Ethan told me this morning to save some of those donuts for you since he knew how much you liked them."

Cali blinked. "He did?"

Ethan's head snapped toward Minka, eyes wide. "I—what?"

Minka only grinned. "Don't be modest, hon. Not many men remember what a woman wants the first time."

She took his order. Breakfast for dinner. Over-easy eggs on corned beef hash, home fries, and buttered toast. Cali liked the sound of that, too. Her mouth watered with hunger already.

"You want apple cider donuts, too, Ethan? They're fresh."

"He does," Cali answered, "if he knows what's good for him."

"Oh, I'm sure he knows what's good for him." And with that, she whisked away before he could protest.

Ethan exhaled, shaking his head with a helpless laugh.

"Don't mind her. She's incorrigible." Cali took a long, satisfying sip of her coffee.

"More like a fairy godmother," said Ethan. "I have to admit, I did *not* know about the donuts, let alone your regular order. All the credit goes to Minka there. But now you've got me curious. What's in that thing?" He pointed at her mug.

As Cali went through the details, she noticed Ethan's face growing increasingly overwhelmed.

"But Minka just calls it my Oat Couture."

Ethan practically spit out his coffee. "That tracks! Highly specific." He lowered his voice and leaned across the table some, forcing Cali to lean closer. "You know, sometimes, when I'm feeling frisky," he said, "I add some creamer to mine."

Cali chortled and hit him softly with her napkin. "Stop mocking me. You know, they don't bat an eye at an order like this in Eastmoor. I'm just glad I found Minka and didn't have to compromise my coffee morals when I moved here."

"So you used to live in Eastmoor? That's a pretty big city.

What brought you to Autumn Ridge?"

From there he kept going, asking more and more—about her old corporate job, the house she inherited from her grandmother, her cat brooches, the library, the recent whereabouts of the Maine Coon, the hotly debated Banned Books Week display she wanted. Each question drew her further in, until she realized she'd been talking for half an hour straight. Ethan hadn't offered much about himself at all. He just sat there, listening like her answers mattered more than anything going on around them.

When she finally looked down, she noticed her sandwich sat nearly untouched. His plate, though, was spotless save for a dab of ketchup at the corner of his mouth.

"What?" he asked, following her eyes to the ketchup spot and wiping it away with his napkin. He cleared his throat. "Why do women do that?"

"Do what?"

"Eat so little on the first date." He gestured down toward her plate. "Nervous?"

She scoffed. "This is *not* a date. And if you hadn't intercepted me on the sidewalk and asked about my entire life, this sandwich would've disappeared 28 minutes ago."

"Then, please, finish. I won't say another word."

He took the bill straight from Minka's hands when she appeared. Receipt signed, he leaned forward, chin resting on his hand as Cali finished her sandwich and donuts. His eyes lingered on her mouth, his own lips twitching like he had something he shouldn't say. He masked it with a slow drag of his thumb along his jaw, but the scruff catching the last of the sun only made the effort look more deliberate, like he was hiding thoughts that didn't belong in the café.

CHAPTER 5

Cali caught herself smiling into her empty mug, her belly warm and full. She wasn't sure which version of Ethan she liked better—the one hanging on every detail of her life or the quiet one watching her now. Either was better than the guy who'd tried to one-up her over a stray cat.

And still, she wanted to know more. What about the cat tail tattooed to his shoulder? Where had he grown up? Why had he taken a job that meant packing up and leaving every couple of years?

But the desire to know made her uneasy. He'd be gone by spring. He wanted her cat. The reasons not to try stacked higher than the ones that did. For now, Ethan Cross was nothing more than a rival at worst, an acquaintance at best. At least, that's what she told herself.

"Thank you for the meal, Ethan. But don't get any ideas. This isn't *coq au vin*."

"Wouldn't dream of it," he said easily, though his gaze didn't quite let her go.

That was her cue. She grabbed her trench, slipped her bag over her shoulder, and rose from the booth, smoothing her skirt as if to prove to herself it really was time to leave.

He stayed seated, watching her with that quiet, steady patience that felt like it could undo her if she lingered another minute.

Outside, the evening air wrapped around her as she walked back toward the library parking lot and under the haze of the streetlights. Only then did she realize, full stomach or not, a different kind of hunger lingered.

Chapter 6

The weekend and most of the week after it went by without fanfare. Texts about the Maine Coon with The Nine and daily library duties kept Cali's mind occupied. But by Thursday's drive into work, her nerves were stricken both with how dangerously close time was creeping toward the library board meeting and with how she'd likely see Ethan again tonight after Book Club.

She fumbled with her keys, skirt swishing in the fresh autumn air as she walked around to the back of the library. She couldn't bring herself to enter through the front doors anymore, couldn't give Ethan the satisfaction of seeing her. If she ever let down her guard again like she had last Friday at Minka's, she didn't know what would happen. Or maybe she knew *exactly* what would happen: He'd hold her gaze just like he had across the diner table, plush lips parted, and eyes intense, and she'd lose all of her words, all her precious wit, just for the chance he'd press those lips against hers. It was too big a risk. Innocent waves across the street and peeks out the window would be like water torture, slowly breaking down her resolve. So she kept her focus on the cats and work and nothing else.

He must've picked up on the change in the air, because he didn't surprise her with his presence again. Or maybe he realized, too, that all this could be was temporary and he didn't want to press it if it didn't come easily.

After feeding the strays in the back and taking inventory of the morning's schedules, Cali made her way to the front door and was distracted by a loud *thud* among the stacks. She froze. It turned quiet, but that sound was enough for concern. She grabbed the closest weapon she could find—a stapler—and tip-toed to where she thought she'd heard it.

In the Occult section, right under *Signs, Omens & Familiars* was the Maine Coon kitten, cuddled against the books. One of its legs dangled over the shelf's edge. Several hardcovers had spilled onto the floor beneath it.

"How on earth did you get in here?" she whispered.

The cat slow-blinked its eyes at her, unfussed, as if it owned the place.

She tip-toed back to her purse, grabbed some cat treats from inside, and made a trail from the shelf to a cardboard cat carrier she kept in her office in case one of the strays ever had an emergency.

A few sniffs in the air and the kitten leapt down and devoured the trail behind her. It was almost too easy.

When it was secured in the carrier, she grabbed her phone and took a photo of a little pink nose peeking through one of the holes. Then she texted The Nine. *Guess who finally showed up at the library?! Mission: Maine Coon—accomplished!*

While texts of congratulations and where and how she found it flooded her screen, Cali noticed an alert appear. A new number added to the chat. Leo's text came next: *Cali caught it, man!*

That was when she realized, *Shit. That must be Ethan's number.*

Another message to the group, from the new number, appeared immediately: *Cute. So is it a he or a she?*

Cali's face soured. She could ignore it, but now that he'd asked, she was sure the rest of them would want to know. If she replied, Ethan would know it was her number. How quickly avoidance had turned into him being involved again. She reminded herself to punch Leo in the arm next time she saw him.

A girl, obviously, Cali texted back. Of course she didn't know for sure. There was all that fluffy fur hiding things, and she didn't dare let it escape again just to check. But she wasn't going to give Ethan the satisfaction of raining on her parade in a group chat either.

I wanna pet the floof tonight! Minka replied. Several of the others agreed. But then an argument ensued over whether or not that many cuddles would be too overwhelming for the stray.

Fortunately, no one mentioned handing the cat over to Ethan. And neither did he. The matter seemed to be settled. They'd all made efforts to find it, and Cali was clearly the one who finally did. Or rather, it had chosen her.

She skated through the rest of the day on a cloud, checking in frequently on the kitten and giving it as much pâté as its heart desired—which was a lot. Even the heavy drilling noises from the excavation couldn't dampen her mood today. By the time the book club was in attendance, it was all they could talk about. Minka brought cookies to celebrate. Lynne brought some beer from her pub. Mrs. Ellery even suggested they postpone the scheduled book discussion for the following week.

With no sight or knock from Ethan by half-past eight, Cali felt her body finally relax. The cat—and the help in finding it—was really all he'd wanted after all. Now that it was hers, he had no reason to come to Nine Lives. No reason to note her daily routine. No reason to, intentional or not, stand shirtless in view of her office window ever again.

But all her hopes were dashed the next minute, when Leo announced Ethan had been hanging around outside for the past ten minutes. He sprinted toward the doors as Freya said, "I guess we were so busy celebrating we didn't hear him."

Ethan followed behind Leo. He wore yet another gray shirt, light and heathered this time, with a V-neck. Cali would have to ask him about all that gray someday. It clung to his deltoids and pecks as he walked, and Cali felt the world tilt toward him for a moment. Heat curled low in her belly, every nerve in her suddenly awake and humming.

"I do have one topic I want to discuss with you all, now that Ethan's here," Mrs. Ellery said. She stretched a hand in his direction lovingly, like a grandmother might. "You're part of this group now, too, Ethan. Before you came, The Nine—as we like to call ourselves—only totaled eight."

Cali hadn't thought of that before. But even as that comforting realization sank in, a little voice reminded her Ethan wouldn't be around forever.

Mrs. Ellery continued. "Since we've saved our first stray as a team, I think it's high time we put our heads together to do more. What would you say to a fundraiser? Or a gala—for the Autumn Ridge strays?" She turned to Cali. "That way you won't have to feed them out of your own pocket for a while. You can focus on feeding the Maine Coon instead."

"What if we used it for food, litter, and vet bills for the fosters, just like a shelter would?" Lynne suggested.

"That's brilliant," said Leo.

"You gotta admit, it's a tempting idea," Freya admitted. Cali could almost see the wheels turning in the florist's head.

Location. Invites. Floral displays, naturally. Minka and Lynne agreed. They could each find some way to contribute.

"I don't own a business," Leo said. "But I could check with the guys at the fire station. I'm sure they'd agree to auction off dates or calendars or something of value."

"Ooh," Lynne said, almost too eagerly. "I like the sound of that!"

"Then it's settled," Mrs. Ellery said. "And with that in mind, I've already reserved the ballroom at The Old Ridge Inn for the first Saturday in October. My sister, rest her soul, was best friends with the owner, Rosita."

Cali stammered out a "What?" in disbelief.

"Which part, my dear?"

"All of it!" said Leo. The Nine nodded their heads in agreement. It was one thing to discuss expanding their efforts and another to do it within a few weeks.

She shrugged. "Well, I figured you'd say yes anyway. No deposit needed because of my sister. Rosita said consider it her donation instead. This should give us plenty of time to advertise and invite people, maybe even some of your connections from Eastmoor." She waved a hand at Cali. "But otherwise, why not? Banned Books Week will be over, if Cali secures it. Fall colors, crisp nights. Perfect for a formal event. Why, even the fall festival will be wrapping up! We'll have everyone's attention—and maybe all their money with it."

"I'm still in if Leo gets the firefighters to auction off dates," said Lynne. "I'll cater the drinks."

Leo smiled until his dimples threatened to cut through his cheeks.

"Then it's settled. We'll make a list of everything that needs to be done and divide and conquer."

"For the cats," added Bastet, raising her beer.

"For the cats!" exclaimed everybody.

Cali shot a shy glance at Ethan, only to find his eyes were already on her.

"I really need to discuss a small matter, too," Cali added, "about the cat sitting in my office. I need some ideas. I called the vet today, and they can't get it in for a check-up until next month ... unless I come tomorrow at 3:30 p.m., during library hours. It's just that one of the staff already called out for tomorrow, so I—"

"I'll take her," Ethan said without hesitation.

She glared at him. "Don't you have beams to measure?" Then she realized her tone and cleared her throat. "Sorry. I'm just a little frustrated. I'll call the vet and beg for a Saturday slot."

He shrugged off the thought of it. "I get cut early this Friday. It's cool. I have all afternoon to be with her."

Another worry crept into Cali's brain. *Is this him trying to get close to my cat again?*

"I know he's the newest member, dear," Mrs. Ellery started, "but let him earn his stripes."

Minka smirked. "Yeah, Cali. Are you scared he'll do it better than you?"

"Of course not." Cali shot her a look that screamed *Chaos goblin!*

"Ethan knows what he's doing. He's already a cat dad," Leo insisted. "Met Catsby last weekend during the game. She's one cool kitty. I'll probably introduce her to Fred some time."

Lynne groaned. "Not unless you want The Great Catsby to turn into the The Great Litter. Fred's a tom. You need to get that cat neutered, Leo."

The subject turned to Leo's cat, and opinions flew again. This could not be any further from the kind of help Cali wanted. "Fine," she interrupted them. "But if she comes back missing fur, I'm holding you all responsible."

When she glanced across at Ethan this time, he was leaning back in his chair, eyes intense and wide, wicked grin on his face.

Chapter 7

The group dispersed after it was all settled, but Minka stayed behind to chat with Cali in her office. She could tell Cali was upset over something, because she'd been fidgety through the whole club meeting. Minka also knew it had nothing to do with the cat.

Cali shuffled papers at her desk. "It's the library board. The meeting's Monday, and I still don't have a plan to counter their rejection to my initial idea for Banned Books Week."

"What problem did they have with your display again?"

"The descriptions," Cali hissed, "which is contrary to the whole point of a banned books display. They wanted me to tone down the publisher's blurb for *Charlotte's Web*, for Christ's sake. I guess calling out our own mortality is a little too much for the board."

Minka rolled her eyes. "That's just because the board's full of old guys close to the grave themselves. Can you revise them?"

"I could," Cali admitted, "but where does it end? They've already started making cuts—said no to *The Handmaid's Tale* because of the slavery and trauma. *The Handmaid's Tale!*" She slammed her hand against the desk. "This isn't even about the descriptions anymore. It's about perception."

Minka bit her lower lip.

A soft knock came at the door. When she stepped aside, Ethan was there, pulling a hand through his dark hair. "Am I interrupting something important?"

Cali groaned, tugging at the mess of papers on her desk. The kitten, still trapped in its cardboard carrier in the corner, meowed in protest.

"Not important enough you two can't talk," Minka said, backing out. "Catch you later, Cals. Text me if I can help." She waved and disappeared.

"I just wondered—" Ethan started.

Cali's glasses slid down her nose as she fumbled with the stack of papers, one slipping to the floor. She bent to retrieve it, but her hands shook, scattering a few more. Ethan lunged forward to help, but she waved him off. "I'm sorry you had to see that."

"I overheard a bit," he mumbled. "Sounds like this is important to you. Sorry the board's giving you such a hard time."

Cali nodded her head. "No one gets how difficult these kinds of discussions can be in a small town. But it's worth it. These books have done nothing wrong! I just want to bring them some visibility."

"Sounds like the board doesn't want that, though."

"Ding, ding, ding." Her voice was flat, jaw clenched, eyes fixed on the scattered papers.

Then she realized she was targeting the wrong guy. She sighed and sank into her desk chair. He slid into the seat across from her. Despite the fluorescent lights and rigid furniture, some of the comfort she'd felt with him last Thursday at the café booth bubbled up in her again. "I'm being a jerk, Ethan. I don't mean to take it out on you. I can't even blame alcohol this time. I didn't touch Lynne's beer stash."

"It's okay. Makes sense you're upset. I read *The Handmaid's Tale* in high school. So did everyone else I know. It's horrific. Don't get me wrong. But everyone should try to read it."

"I appreciate that." The air felt heavy between them. "What was on your mind, though? Hopefully not the library board."

"Just a quick question. Drop off and pickup for the vet tomorrow: the library?" He paused, catching his bottom lip between his teeth. "Or your place?"

"My place?"

"You said your place is out by the lake, right? The vet's office is halfway between here and there. I could head either direction."

She paused to think. Had he really remembered that from their chat last week? She brushed off the thought, nodding her head briskly, but it lingered nonetheless. "Well, I suppose I could bring her into work tomorrow and let you take it from there. I don't get out of here until 6 p.m. on Fridays, though, so—"

"So I'll meet you at your place."

The look between them settled and deepened. Cali imagined him on her doorstep, the fading red sunset against his back, and how she already knew in her gut this was a very bad idea. The worst. But like watching a slow-motion car crash, she felt helpless to stop it.

She scribbled out the address of the A-frame and passed it across the table to him. His hands clung to it like it was a map out of the desert.

"One more thing," he said.

"No, I will not settle your overdue fines just because you're helping with the cat."

He let out a startled laugh and shook his head. "Well, you can't blame a guy for trying. Good to know you're up on my bad-boy patron file, though." He gave her the side-eye. "I intend to pay those soon. But, seriously. This library board, I think you can beat them at their own game—literally."

"What do you mean?"

"Instead of your original proposal, why don't you gamify it? Like, create a scavenger-hunt-style display throughout the library. Each book would have its summary or 'reason it was challenged' written in invisible ink. Patrons can check out a small UV pen from the desk to reveal the message. It's educational, but it feels more like a game." Cali's interest was piqued. "You're showing respect for all patrons and the board by letting people choose how much to engage. No changing the descriptions. No striking books from your list. It's just there if they want to participate."

Cali crinkled her nose in thought. "Invisible ink, huh? The board might faint on the spot. On the other hand ..." She bit the inside of her cheek, already filing it away. But she couldn't let Ethan see just how much space he was taking up in her head—and her library. "I'll think about it."

"Fair enough. I just thought it might give you another angle." He wrung his hands together, pushed his fingers through his wavy hair, and rose from his seat. "I guess I'll get going. See you here at 3:15 p.m. tomorrow?"

"Sure. If I'm busy, just ask at the front desk. I'll let them know you're coming, and the cat will be here in my office."

He gave a slight wave of his hand on his way out and closed the door behind him.

Cali cracked open another can of pâté and watched the Maine Coon kitten eat it on her desk. The fluffy ball of chocolate and smoke-colored fur was ravenous, and for a moment she felt bad about not letting it out to say hello to Ethan, too. When it was done, it gazed up at her, eyes like polished marbles, deep and wondering, then crawled into her lap and purred.

She remembered this feeling. She'd missed it so much, and now it was finally part of her world again. A tear slipped free, unseen but for the kitten, as she stroked its fur. Still, her mind kept circling around the one question she didn't dare ask: Ethan Cross—rival, rescuer, or something far more risky?

Chapter 8

After a night of cuddles in bed together, the Maine Coon kitten seemed calmer at the library the next day. However, the minute any of the staff caught wind of their new guest, they had to visit Cali's office, which meant a revolving door of visitors on one of the busiest days of the week.

By the time Ethan arrived for the vet appointment pickup, she was behind and torn between three competing priorities. Consistency checks became a rabbit hole, and a simple story time event was complicated by unexpected turnout and accessibility needs. She couldn't even meet him at the front desk. So, as promised, one of the staff led him back to collect the little furball.

When she finally found a moment to breathe and refresh her coffee in her office, one of her co-workers, Russell, appeared in her doorway. "Cali," he said sternly, "you did *not* warn us about that man who came to pick up your new kitten."

Cali's mind raced with all that could have gone wrong. Had Ethan insulted someone in an effort to be cute? Had he been demanding, or worse, aloof? The staff always kept an eye out for dangerous people in public spaces. She hung her head. "Oh no. What did he say?"

"Nothing. But *you* failed to tell us how hot this guy was going to be. Bernadette nearly passed out on the circulation desk."

"For crying out loud, guys."

"Is he yours?" he asked.

Cali nearly spit her coffee back into her Purride and Purrjudice mug. "Ethan?"

"Who else? Have you been holding out on us? And here I thought we were all like family."

"Russell, he is *not* my boyfriend. And I've got a lot of work to do still before 6 p.m. So if you don't mind." She waved a hand toward the door.

"Right. So the six-foot-tall Superman lookalike—whom you have no interest in —volunteers to bring your new rescue—who was putty in his hands, by the way—to the vet while you're at work. Because. It's. Completely. Platonic."

"Russ!"

"Nope. Got it. Cool cool cool. I'm just trying to avoid a crisis here. Bernadette's zhuzhing up her makeup in the unisex bathroom, anticipating his return as we speak. If she doesn't stand a chance, I need to know now. You *saw* how she cried at the end of *La La Land*."

Cali cleared her throat. "He's not dropping off the cat here."

"He's not?"

She shifted uncomfortably in her seat. "No, he's dropping it off at my place." Russell stared, gape-mouthed, at her for several moments. "Out!" she demanded.

He turned indignantly and shut the door behind him.

That conversation with Russell was all she could think about as she drove home on the winding, painted-leaf streets back to the lake. It was all she could think about when she spotted Ethan's truck already sitting in her driveway, him standing just outside his door, the kitten calm and out of its carrier and cuddled in his large hands. It wasn't fleeing at all. It was thoroughly enjoying head scratches when she rolled up and parked the car in front of them.

Ethan was wearing dark jeans and another gray Henley, as though he'd ordered them in bulk just to torment her.

"Do you have a thing for gray?" she asked him. "Or are you secretly colorblind?"

"I've been told it brings out my eyes," he teased.

She pointed at the cat, which he'd yet to hand over. "Well, at least you and the cat match today. But don't go getting any ideas. She chose me. Remember?"

"Oh, by the way," Ethan said, stealing his gaze momentarily from the cat snuggled in his arms, "your girl is a boy."

Cali's mouth dropped open. She was mortified, especially after bragging in the group chat. "Well, you could've texted me that!" she scoffed.

"But then I'd miss your reaction," Ethan countered. "Priceless." He served her a smile, lips curved wide, teeth flashing, but it was the crinkle at the corners of his eyes that made the smile feel real. Ethan was handsome already, but when he smiled like that, he became positively devastating.

Ethan cuddled the nearly-asleep cat into the carrier again, passed it into her hands, and walked with her until she reached her front door.

Cali fumbled with her keys while balancing the carrier. Ethan's hand shot out before she could protest, steadying the box as she nudged the door open. The kitten gave a pitiful mewl.

"Relax, you're home," Ethan murmured down at it, then glanced up at her with that infuriating half-smile. "You sure you don't want me to help you get him inside?"

CHAPTER 8

"I've managed fine with cats and doors for years," she said, taking the carrier back once they stepped into the kitchen. Still, the way his presence filled the threshold made her pulse kick.

He lingered a moment longer, leaning against the doorframe, as she released the kitten from its box. She opened a can of cat food and coaxed it over, and Ethan watched as the kitten dove into its dish like it hadn't eaten in weeks. She petted its back and its purr kicked into gear. Ethan's thumb grazed his jaw.

"Lucky little guy," he said softly and paused. "Speaking of lucky ... you doing anything tonight?"

Cali narrowed her eyes, though she couldn't stop the curve of her mouth. "You're insufferable."

"Maybe. But your hair is already washed and perfect. You have no more excuses. And look at him." He pointed down at the kitten. "The little guy is so tired after that appointment, he'll be curled up in your bed and conked out long before you get home."

Cali crossed her arms and nervously fiddled with the button at the top of her polka dot cardigan. "What did you have in mind?" she asked.

He shoved his hands in his pockets, suddenly appearing nervous. "I wondered if you wanted to hit up the Fall Festival. I've never been. But if I just get back in my truck and go hang out with Catsby, I'll miss my chance."

Had he spoken to Leo? How did he know the Fall Festival was her catnip? Had Minka let that slip one morning?

It sounded casual. But the look on his face didn't seem casual at all. Ethan Cross was standing in her doorway. Not a parking lot. Not at the library. And he was trying his damnedest not to seem too hopeful as he waited for her answer. She was dangerously close to admitting Russell might've been right about Ethan's intentions.

She sighed. "Give me ten minutes to freshen up. You wait in the truck, not in here."

"Yes, ma'am," he said, saluting her as he walked back over to his truck.

She closed the door and leaned her forehead against it. Ten minutes. That was barely enough time to freshen her lipstick, let alone learn how to play with fire.

Chapter 9

If one thing was clear, it was that Ethan's truck was a mess. He'd cleared just enough space on the passenger side for a cat carrier—or possibly Cali—to fit, while the floor was littered with grease-smeared rags, crumpled receipts, and more of those damn tape measures.

He was still scrambling to make it presentable when the ten minutes were up. "Hadn't really thought this part through," he insisted. "It's been a long time since I had a guest in here." He swept the last of the clutter into a cardboard box and slid it into the truck bed. "There," he said with a grin. "Should be good now."

When Cali climbed in, she noticed the seat stretched in one continuous sweep of gray cloth from door to door—a bench seat, probably refurbished but softened with time. The kind that ran clear across, smooth and wide, with nothing between them. No console or cup holders. Though she imagined, since there was no headrest behind the middle, it probably folded down for an armrest.

She folded her mauve skirt beneath her and settled in, the faint smell of motor oil filling the cab. "How old is your truck?" she asked curiously. "Reminds me of one my grandpa used to own. No bucket seats."

"Yep," he said. "It's old. I've been eyeing some newer models, but they just don't make them like these anymore."

The engine coughed to life, low and familiar. As they pulled out of her driveway, Ethan rolled the windows down, letting the night air tumble through. A hint of woodsmoke drifted from scattered chimneys. Mailboxes leaned at odd angles along the winding road, their numbers fading, pumpkins and cornstalks tied to a few fence posts. Glimpses of the lake behind them flashed like hammered silver through the trees.

"Leo took me fishing out here a few times this summer," Ethan said. "Feels like you people live inside a dream."

He wasn't wrong. Autumn Ridge had always been that for her. First as a child visiting her grandmother, now as the only place she could imagine calling home. She had a house, a job, friends, The Nine, even a cat again. So why was she testing perfection with a man who could be nothing more than a fling and then off to the next construction project? It's not like she hadn't had a fling before. She'd had a few. But those came at a time when her heart seemed to bounce back faster than it could these days.

Maybe she didn't know what she wanted. But when she turned from the window and caught Ethan stealing a glance, the heat prickling over her skin told her one thing: she wanted more of that.

He parked the truck, and the minute Cali opened the door, her ears were filled with the low murmur of townsfolk greeting each other by name. Strings of twinkling lights crisscrossed overhead, and the sweet, buttery aroma of kettle corn found her nose.

They stood at the entrance side-by-side but then started walking in opposite directions.

"Where are you going?" he asked. "The ring toss is this way."

CHAPTER 9

"To the palm reader, of course," Cali said.

Their eyes narrowed at each other.

"You'd rather waste money on predictions than let me win you a prize at one of these games?"

"Ha! If you think you can win anything." She rolled her eyes. "Don't you know those games are rigged to take your money?"

Ethan smirked. "Okay, Jacobs. Let's do this fair and square. You humor me with one game, I'll humor you with one fortune."

She conceded, and he put a hand around the small of her back and led her in his direction. Whether from fear she'd escape or something else, that hand lingered until they stood in front of Pop-a-Pumpkin, a tall board painted with pumpkins in a pile, orange balloons tethered to the front. The game attendant swung by with enough darts for them both.

"Perfect test of focus and precision," Ethan said. "Let me show you how it's done."

He launched one dart, and it bounced right off one of the balloons, not even breaking the surface. The second dart lodged into the clear blue sky painted on the board's background. The third one sailed over the top.

He turned with a sheepish smile toward Cali.

"What happened to hand-eye coordination, Mr. Construction?" she teased. "Glad I didn't have my heart set on anything."

"Guess I'm not as focused as I thought. Best two out of three?" he asked.

"Won't be necessary."

She raised one dart to the level of her glasses, closed an eye, and directed it at the board. A fat *pop* sounded as it struck a balloon in the dead-center of the pile. She repeated the motions, securing two more wins. A few of the other gamers clapped for her.

She turned to Ethan and found the balloons weren't the only thing deflated.

"But how ... ?" he muttered in awe of her. "You said these things were rigged."

"Right, and I know the tricks from a book I read at the library." She turned to the clothesline of toys to choose from. "What do you want?"

For the next several minutes, Ethan clutched a brown and orange hoot-owl plushie between his hands as they wound through the vendor stalls. Cali tried not to laugh. He murmured something about how much Catsby would enjoy the owl, trying not to chuckle as well.

The cheerful swell of a bluegrass band tuned up in the distance, mingled with bursts of laughter. Kids darted past with candy apples, faces sticky and bright. One of them ran up and gave Ethan a high-five, as if they knew each other. The kid's dad, Tom, one of the town's realtors, greeted Ethan with a smile.

"Ethan! Didn't I just see you up on Mrs. Porter's roof last weekend?" he asked.

Ethan shrugged. "Just a couple shingles."

Cali's brows shot up. First Leo. Then diners at the café. Now the festival. How did he already know everyone in Autumn Ridge? She'd been here a couple years permanently and still felt like an outsider at times.

As they waited in line for the palm reader, Cali rocked back and forth on her heels, her mauve skirt playing between her legs and his.

"You okay?" he asked. "I'm sure she's paid to keep a positive spin on it."

CHAPTER 9

"Just getting a little cool," Cali admitted. "I didn't think to bring a coat."

Ethan glanced down at the plushie and up at her and down at the plushie again. "One sec," he said and ran off.

When he returned, the plushie was gone and he was extending a wool-lined jean jacket in her direction. The shoulders were way too broad for her. She practically swam in it, but it was a relief to cozy up inside the coat. It smelled exactly like Ethan, a mix of sweet and spicy. She found herself blushing at the gesture.

Ethan saddled up beside her this time, his arm softly grazing against hers, and crossed his arms over his chest. His forearms flexed beneath the Henley. She hated how her gaze lingered, how such a simple gesture could bring heat to her cheeks.

"Aren't you getting cold, too?" she asked.

The twinkling lights above them danced. "I'll be fine," he said. But the wind kicked up, and she noticed his grip tighten. "Maybe we can grab some hot cider after this, though?"

"Deal."

The palm reader's tent was smaller than she'd remembered. The three of them crowded under the draped purple and gold fabric, faces lit up by the pink hue of a crystal ball in between them. Ethan's knee brushed against hers under the table, warm and firm. If she dared move away, her chair might topple over.

The palmist read them separately then together, explaining the right hand reflected the present and future, while the left hand was their pasts. She picked up on Ethan's frequent travels, his long heart line. "Your fate line shows constant change. You're not one to stay still. But your heart line runs deep. When you choose to love, it's steady—you don't give it lightly."

"And you," she said, turning toward Cali. "You're more

anchored. Home means everything. But here—see the dip? You've been hurt. You don't let just anyone in."

The palmist placed their hands beside each other then. "Lovers?" she asked, so casually it caught them both off guard. But she shook her head before they could answer. "Ah, rivals ... but not for long. Everything will work out if both of you really want it to."

Their eyes met across the crystal ball, and for once, neither of them had a clever retort.

Chapter 10

It wasn't until they were seated alone at a bench, hot cider cupped in their hands, that Ethan started prying. "So 'anchored,' huh? Is that how you really feel about Autumn Ridge?"

Cali had to admit it was. She told him how, even before her grandmother had willed her the house, her family had driven down for this exact same fall festival each year. And the holidays. And the spring flower event. And the Fourth of July. "Where do you think I get all these brooches?" she asked, pointing at the sparkling white one pinned to her chest. "They sell them at a booth right over there. I'm obsessed."

"Must be nice," he said, "having a place like this, a place that feels like home."

Cali smiled. "You know, it's like those swallows, in Capistrano. Doesn't matter how far they go, they always circle back. That's Autumn Ridge for me." She took a long sip of her cider.

Ethan stared past her, deep in thought, then said, "When I was a kid, my older sister and I lived with our mom in Miami. She was single, worked as a realtor. She was barely home, so we had a lot of time to get into trouble." He chuckled softly, remembering but not sharing. "When my mom remarried, my stepdad was military, so we moved every couple years. New schools, new towns, no time to get attached. Guess I got used to not feeling tied down. After a while, moving was just easier, starting over in a new place," he said with a half-smile. "When you never unpack all the way, there's not much to lose when it's time to go."

Cali watched him for a beat, the lights from the cider tent flickering across his face.

"Ah. So that's how you've gotten to know people here so quickly. You're used to it."

Ethan gave her a puzzled expression. "Well, there's more to it than that."

"How so?"

Cali tilted her head, waiting, but before he could explain, a shriek of laughter split the air. A cluster of kids rushed a barrel, dunking their heads beneath the water. Ethan blinked at the chaos.

"What is this insanity?"

"You've never bobbed for apples? It's basically a rite of passage around here. Miami didn't have bobbing for apples?"

"Miami didn't even have fall. We had year-round summer ... and hurricanes."

She crinkled her nose at that. "So no corn mazes, no cider, no pumpkin contests?"

"Closest thing I had was chasing ice cream trucks." The twinkling lights played against his hair and cheekbones. "You know, I really admire how sure you are of yourself here, how comfortable. You belong in a way I've never truly felt."

If only he knew. Yes, she knew Autumn Ridge like the back of her hand, thanks to all those childhood visits to her grandmother. But the town didn't quite know her yet. And sometimes she wondered if that was her fault. A pang of guilt flickered as she thought of how easily people waved and spoke to Ethan, how even the stray kitten had gravitated to him first. She only had it now because luck or fate had sent it through the library doors on a cold night.

"That's just small-town living," she muttered. "Nothing special."

Ethan put his cup aside and scooted toward her on the bench, the full span of his muscular thigh pressed against her skirt. She felt the warmth radiating off him and suddenly felt dizzy, like on the Tilt-a-Whirl. All euphoric and off-center. Ethan's gaze fell to her lips and lingered there. "No. It *is* special. Cali, don't you see? You're—"

A harsh voice cut through the crowd. "Cross! There you are." A stocky man clapped Ethan on the shoulder. In his other hand he gripped a smoked turkey leg. "They're pulling the raffle for Sutton's Auto Body. Free oil change. Whole crew's headed that way. You in?"

Cali couldn't be sure, but between the gruffness and his appearance, she thought this might be the foreman—the one Minka complained about.

Ethan turned his head, somewhat perturbed, then glanced back at Cali. "Hey, Carl. Meet Cali. She's a ... uh ... she's a friend."

Carl gave her a quick nod. "Nice to meet you." Then his attention was back on Ethan. "So you in or what?"

"I'm kind of in the middle of something right now, Carl. But let me know if one of the guys wins, okay? I'll catch you after the weekend."

The foreman took a bite of the turkey leg, juice running down his hand, and talked as he chewed. "Right. Oh, remind me to ask you on Monday about scheduling the flatbed move, will ya? Time's tickin'. Guess we'll barely wrap Autumn Ridge before we're on the road again."

Ethan shifted his weight back, one hand raking through his dark hair, and tried desperately to catch Cali's eye again. But she didn't notice. Her stomach was already tightening at the words. *On the road again.* She forced a polite smile and excused herself to a trash can to throw away her cup while the two of them finished talking. The carnival music hung in the air, tinny and bright, at odds with the weight in Cali's chest.

When she returned to the bench, she didn't even bother to sit down again. She burrowed into his coat, hands in pockets, and said, "Maybe we should get going."

Ethan let out a long sigh. "I'm sorry. Carl's not good at reading the room. I had no idea he'd be here."

"It's okay," she said, shaking her head. "I think I'm just getting tired. Usually I'm half asleep in front of the TV by now, bowl of popcorn in my lap. Kind of eager to get home to that little fluffball anyway."

"Okay," he said, and he rose from the bench. They walked back to the parking lot together, a chill nestling into Cali's bones.

Back at her place, Ethan insisted on walking her the few yards from his truck to the door. The autumn air was in full effect and alive with the subtle, layered sounds of hooting owls and katydids singing. The wind picked up, making the wind chime hanging beside her doorstep dance with its soft, rhythmic tings. She breathed in deeply, relishing the feeling of that post-fall festival glow.

"Well, thanks for tonight," she said, unlocking the door and turning back toward Ethan. "And for helping me feel better about my dart skills."

She could tell he was relieved to hear her being playful again, relaxed instead of uptight and quiet, as she'd been the entire ride back home. He smiled down at her, his gray eyes tracing her features. Hair and eyes, then finally landing on her lips. "Do you think she's right about us? The palmist?" he asked. "Rivals, but not for long?"

"Only if we both really want it," she reminded him. "Do you really want it, Ethan?"

He smirked and stepped closer. "I do. I really want it. But do me a favor and check over my shoulder for hidden Carls this time, okay?"

Her heels lifted just enough to peer over his broad shoulders and catch the scent of his hair. But he couldn't wait any longer. He leaned down and brushed his lips against hers, her body lifting toward him. His lips still tasted like apple cider. A soft moan escaped her, so he deepened the kiss, hands pressed into the small of her back. Next thing she knew, her fingertips were touching his jawline and pulling through his hair, like satin against her skin. The sensation unraveled her. She was shocked at how natural it felt, to connect with him, to feel completely consumed.

Ethan paused to come up for air and grazed his lips along her cheek and earlobe. A shudder ran down Cali's spine.

"I shouldn't say this," he whispered, "but ... you in these skirts? It drives me crazy."

"Really?" she whispered back.

He nodded. "You've got no idea, do you? How good you look when you're not even trying?"

He wasn't wrong. Cali never saw herself as, well, *attractive*. Sure, she was put together nicely. Nice clothes and nice makeup. But she wasn't the kind of woman men went out of their way to pursue. That was reserved for young blondes in shorter skirts than she'd ever wear. When guys were attracted to her, it was usually because of her wit or intelligence. And she didn't mind that at all. In fact, she was almost certain Ethan was attracted to those qualities, too. But no one had ever said she drove them crazy before.

Ethan traced the tip of his nose down her neck, kissing there too, nipping and sucking until she thought she might melt right into the porch. *Damn you, Ethan Cross.* She hated how easily he undid her. She touched his chin and guided his lips back to hers.

She didn't want this night to end, yet the words "Pretty sure this breaks some kind of library rule" slipped out against his mouth. "You know—falling for the patrons. Maybe we should call it a night."

"Is this about my overdue library fines?" he murmured. "I've got money in the truck. I'll pay you back right now."

She giggled, and he shuddered at the feel of her breath against his skin.

"Okay. If you want to stop here, we stop. Call me a vampire, but I don't cross the threshold unless you say so." Ethan kissed her once more, firm and unhurried, but he didn't let her go.

God, it was tempting. All she had to do was step aside, let him in, give herself over to this ache. But a part of her held back. He wanted more. She could feel it in the quick, unsteady thrum of his heartbeat. She wanted more, too. A *lot* more. But this was already farther than she'd ever intended to go.

She forced herself to step back. "Goodnight, Ethan," she whispered, handing him his coat.

Inside, Cali pressed her back to the door, willing her breath to steady, telling herself she'd done the right thing.

Outside, Ethan lingered on the porch, coat in hand, telling

himself it was right, too—because when she finally let him in, he wanted it to be because she'd chosen to.

Chapter 11

Cali woke Sunday with her stomach in knots, and for once it wasn't because of Ethan. The board meeting loomed like a storm cloud, and she hated the thought that she might've jeopardized her case for Banned Books Week by letting herself get distracted with a kiss on the porch. A kiss she refused to replay in her head—except, of course, she was. Constantly.

Her phone buzzed.

Our Maine Coon still in one piece?

She snorted. *Our.* Probably meant The Nine. Still, it warmed something inside her.

The kitten stretched in a patch of sun beneath the window, paws curled over his pale belly. She snapped a photo, hit send, and texted: *Max.* Then she muted the phone before Ethan could turn it into anything more. She had work to do.

By afternoon, she'd pulled Minka into emergency duties at the library, even though it was closed. Her best friend entrusted her best waitress to man the café while she plopped two Oat Coutures on Cali's desk.

"One for now, one for tomorrow morning. You're obviously not sleeping tonight."

"Have I told you you're my favorite friend?"

"Only every time I see you." Minka folded her arms, squinting at Cali's note cards. "Okay. Hit me with your spiel. I'll be the scary board."

They tried a few rounds. Cali fumbled, reworked, tried again. Minka was ruthless, dramatic, occasionally ridiculous, but between laughs she kept steering Cali back to her points.

Finally, Minka leaned on the desk, eyes narrowed. "Wait. You said Ethan came up with this UV trick?"

Cali froze mid-sip. "Yeah."

Minka shot her a sideways glance. "And you didn't think to ask him to help you rehearse?"

"It's not like we know each other that well."

Minka drummed her fingers lightly on the table as if waiting for more. Cali's cheeks began to blush. "Is it hot in here?" she asked.

"Oh my God. Something happened. Didn't it? I knew it! Tom said he saw you two at the fall festival on Friday."

Damn this town.

"It's nothing." Cali stared into her cup. "Just—" She cut herself off before the words *an earth-shattering kiss* could escape. "He dropped off the cat, and neither of us had anything to do. So we went."

"Uh-huh. Because that's how people usually end up together on a Friday night ... I'm bored. You're bored. Let's ride the Ferris wheel and make out."

"It wasn't like that. We didn't ride the Ferris wheel."

Minka leaned forward, eyes narrowed. "You're holding out on me. Best friends are supposed to share this stuff, Cals. Otherwise how am I supposed to live vicariously through your bad decisions?"

Bad decisions was the understatement of the year. "You're right, okay? We went to the fall festival together and he dropped me off at my place and, yes, there might have been a kiss, but—"

Minka squealed and jumped up from her chair. "Why didn't you say that first?! Who cares about the board. *This* is breaking news! Special report!"

"No. Sit, sit. Stop it!" she chastised. "I didn't tell you because it's nothing more than that. A kiss. I've made my home here. He's leaving. So I'm not letting it go any further." Even as she said those words, she felt a hollow ache open in her middle.

"Damn, Cals. I commend your restraint, but I'm not buying it. You were embroiled in a custody battle over a stray cat last week. Now you're making out on your porch. You do realize you're living in an enemies-to-lovers fanfic, right?"

Cali groaned and buried her face in her hands. "You're impossible." She gathered the stack of notes on the table, deliberately ending the subject. Because if she kept talking about it, she might admit how much she wanted it to happen again. "Board meeting. Tomorrow. That's what matters."

Minka pressed her lips together, unconvinced. "Well then don't make it a whole 'thing.' Keep it a 'fling.' No one's judging you. In fact, several of us might be rooting for you. I know you're at your best when you're a woman with a purpose, Cals. But sometimes the whole purpose can be to have fun."

Cali's eyes narrowed at her. "Don't go orchestrating anything, Minka. I'm serious. No meddling. We both saw right through that 'he knows your order' attempt at the café."

"I can't make any promises on behalf of the universe," Minka sighed. "But fine. I'll behave."

That night, Cali slid into bed with her notes stacked neatly by the lamp. Max curled against her side, purring so hard he vibrated the sheets. She could get used to this.

The phone buzzed one last time on her nightstand. *Good*

luck tomorrow. She didn't need to check the name, but she did anyway. Ethan Cross. Bold letters across the screen, like he was daring her not to reply.

She stretched out a hand to turn off her lamp, careful not to wake Max curled beside her.

Chapter 12

Monday dawned with no room for distractions, though Ethan's good luck text had lodged itself in her brain like a bookmark—distinct enough to keep pulling her attention toward it yet easy enough to pause and leave it where it belonged. The library board would gather in less than an hour, and every word she'd practiced with Minka had to count. Unlike Ethan, they weren't likely to be charmed by a cocky smile.

Max batted at her shoelaces as she dressed for the board meeting, purring like nothing could go wrong. She wished she had his confidence. She buttoned her cardigan, smoothed out her skirt, and headed for the library.

Her palms sweated as she gripped the UV light in front of the five-member board. But her voice was steady while giving her speech. She knew their personalities well already—the naysayer, the ally, the swing voter, and the Board Chair, who'd often stay quiet throughout meetings only to deliver one ego-crushing question at the end. Between that and Minka's ridiculous role-playing yesterday, Cali was more than prepared.

The naysayer cleared his throat, smug. "Why not stick to classics we can all agree on? *Little House on the Prairie* never offended anyone."

Cali steadied her breath. "Even *Little House* has been challenged for its portrayals of Native Americans. The point isn't avoiding offense, it's showing people how complicated history and literature really are."

A few raised brows. A murmur. She pressed on, demonstrating how patrons would need to check out the UV lights to read the descriptions. When the ally said, "Frankly, I admire the creativity here. This makes the display more engaging," she felt the tide turn in her favor.

Then the Board Chair leaned forward, hands folded. "My concern, Ms. Jacobs, is this: If we approve your event once, what's to stop the library from becoming a battleground for every cause? Why should we risk that precedent?"

Cali swallowed hard. "You're right, Chairman Hargrove. Precedent matters—and I love this library as much as you do. That's why I'm not asking for a permanent change or even a policy. I'm asking for *one week*. Banned Books Week is nationally recognized, and this display is about awareness, not division. If it doesn't educate, I'll be the first to admit it failed. And I'll never propose it again."

Silence stretched. The naysayer huffed. The others exchanged glances.

"All in favor?" Hargrove asked.

Four hands rose.

Cali nearly sagged with relief. She'd won. And with all the work she'd put into the demonstration, it would be easy to set up the game. All she had to do now was explain it to the staff, so they were prepared for Banned Books Week next week.

A thrill pulsed through her as she thanked the board and scurried toward her office. She grabbed her phone and texted The Nine.

The board said yes! Banned Books Week is a go!

The Nine drowned her screen in emojis, gifs, and congrats. Minka even promised to update the café menu board with a new latte dubbed *Library Hero*.

She was grinning from the chaos when another message buzzed through, quiet and separate.

Knew you'd nail it. Want to celebrate? —Ethan.

She pressed her lips together, willing herself not to grin. *Sounds like you've got a thing for celebrating. Which do you like more: Celebrations or the color gray?* she texted back.

He thought about it for a while, those triple dots appearing then disappearing.

Celebrating in gray with you sounds just about perfect. Your place tonight? I'll cook.

Heat licked up her neck, blooming beneath her collar. *Cook what?* Cali texted.

Coq au vin, of course.

She ran a hand along her collarbone as Minka's words ran through her head. Maybe she could, against her better judgment, keep things casual with Ethan.

Something caught her eye, and when she turned to her window, she caught him leaning against a tree, hard hat dangling from his hand, his head bent over his phone. She could watch him unseen, and for a second, she let herself.

She typed before she could stop herself: *But that would make it a date.*

Across the lot, his smile spread like a man who'd just won a bet.

Yes, it would. —Ethan.

"Cross! Break time's over. Get moving!" the foreman barked. Ethan jolted, tucked his phone away, and hurried off.

She giggled and pulled the blinds shut.

CHAPTER 12

A few minutes later, her phone buzzed again. *What time's good for you? Any food aversions? Red or white wine? Do you have a pot with a lid? A ladle?*

When she teased him—*Neediest chef I've ever met*—he only replied: *Worth it.*

Chapter 13

That evening, about 15 minutes before Ethan arrived, Cali reapplied her velvety red lipstick in her bathroom mirror and remembered the taste of cider on Ethan's lips from last Friday. Her breath caught in her chest, and she kept having to remind herself *It's just dinner, Cali. Like Minka said, it's supposed to be fun. Relax.*

She wondered, though, if that kiss happened again, what his lips might taste like tonight. And that's as far as she would allow herself to think. Sure, there was that voice in her head saying she was making a mistake. That no good could come from this. Or at least not the good she was used to. Not the routine, reliable kind of good. Hot, sexy, temporary good? Yes. Make-her-moan good? Possibly. Something that left her smiling for days after? Definitely.

But what happened after that was out of her comfort zone—and out of her control. Come the holidays, Ethan would be packed or already gone. And just like she didn't owe him anything after tonight's dinner, he didn't owe her either. If she set her expectations low, then she couldn't get hurt. She'd done the math. At 32, the amount of pain she'd feel when Ethan Cross disappeared from Autumn Ridge and her life could never compare to the kind of pain she'd already survived.

In the full-length mirror, she ran her hands down her cozy yet feminine autumn ensemble—deep burgundy, cropped, button-front cardigan, a mustard-yellow skirt that was a little too short for work, and opaque black tights that ran up her thighs.

She moved around the kitchen, trying to bleed off the nervous energy, opening windows, knowing how warm the kitchen could make the rest of the A-frame feel while in use. Max followed her with a curious glint in his eyes, especially when the field crickets chirped outside.

"Don't go getting ideas, Mister," she warned him with a waggle of her finger.

He crouched down and rolled over onto his back, big turquoise eyes staring up at her innocently.

"I don't believe you, you rascal," she told him.

A knock sounded at the door, and Cali slid through the kitchen in her stocking feet, a faint hum of anticipation running through her veins. She opened the door, and the porch light bled around Ethan. He looked soft and unreal, like a fever dream. Bruised sky against his back, the last light flickering through amber oaks. Sleeves pushed up. Hair damp from the chill. He wore a gray-blue Henley, blue enough to match the dusk. His arms cradled a pot stuffed with kitchen utensils, both hips hugged by bags of groceries.

"May I?" he said with a smirk.

"Oh, shit. Sorry. Yes. Come in."

The cold air carried toward them, damp with the smell of woodsmoke and fallen leaves. Cali's breath fogged as she exhaled. She moved aside, closed the door, and helped Ethan unpack after he set it all down on the countertop.

Her kitchen was narrow and old-fashioned, like a hallway with cabinets and equipment running along its sides. Far too small for both to be in it, their bodies knocking into each other clumsily.

Then Ethan spotted Max. His voice hitched up. "Hey, little guy!" He bent down, and although Max froze in place for a moment, Ethan extended a fist toward him, and the kitten happily plodded over. Ethan cradled Max in his arms as Cali unpacked the last utensil.

"You want me to get something started," Cali offered, "while you two get reacquainted?"

"Nah." He rubbed Max's belly and a loud purr echoed up to the ceiling. "I poured you a glass of wine, by the sink." He nodded his head in that direction. "Your only job tonight is to sit and relax."

Cali didn't want to admit how comforting that sounded. After the build-up toward her case for Banned Books Week, she needed as few obligations as possible tonight. Even her coworkers told her to take tomorrow off after she shared the good news. She deserved it. They had the library covered. Even if things slightly fell apart in her absence, she could put it back together come Wednesday.

She traipsed back to the kitchen and lifted the red wine glass to her lips and felt her muscles relax.

"It's the same wine in the *coq au vin*," Ethan said, nuzzling Max's nose with his. "So it pairs well. Like a sensory bridge between appetizer and dinner."

"Sensory bridge," she murmured against her glass. "Fancy."

He glanced over his shoulder and placed Max on the carpet. "Oh, and I made you, like, a 'charcuterie for one' plate. In case you wanted to nibble beforehand." He walked back to the fridge and handed her a plate she hadn't even noticed him unpack in the chaos of bags, pots, and pans. "This dish could take a while to simmer."

She stared down at the paper plate, flowers printed along the rim. Thin-sliced prosciutto, a small handful of red grapes, brie cheese, and candied pecans stared back. She popped one of the grapes into her mouth and chewed. "How thoughtful of you."

Ethan raised an eyebrow and tried to pull his gaze from her lips. "Have all the other men who've cooked for you failed to provide an appetizer?"

She shimmied past him and slipped onto one of the two chairs at the high-top table that overlooked her garden. Her stocking feet dangled above the floor, and as she devoured a candied pecan, she was taken back to her childhood. All the times when she felt taken care of in this kitchen, all the times someone else had to be in charge. "You are, indeed, the first."

"First one with an appetizer?" he asked, somewhat astonished. The bacon on the stove began to pop and fizz. "Point one for me."

"No," she clarified, "first one to cook me dinner."

"Well," he said, running a thumb over his jaw, "that's gotta be worth at least 10 points."

"I'll be sure to add it to your scorecard at the end of the night."

Ethan navigated her tiny kitchen like he'd lived there for years, sleeves rolled, forearms flexing, the scent of wine and garlic filling the whole room. She smiled at him, the warmth from the oven curling through the air between them. She felt completely relaxed watching him in the moment. Still, her heart seemed to skip a beat when Ethan approached her with a fork pierced through a tiny portion of bacon, his hand cupped underneath.

"I'll need a taste-tester. You up for the task?"

She faked a whine. "I thought you said my only job was to

relax." But she put down the charcuterie plate and opened her mouth just wide enough for him to slip the bacon between her lips. When she bit down, a savory crisp and flash of juicy, smoky flavor filled her cheeks. She leaned back and covered her mouth as she chewed. His fork still hovered between them. "What on earth did you do to that bacon?"

His face fell. "Something wrong?"

"God, no. It's the best bacon I've ever had. Are you sure you didn't buy, like, unicorn meat?"

One of those devastating, eye-wrinkling grins broke across his face. "Add those points to the scorecard, too, then."

He returned to the stove, still grinning from ear to ear, and let Cali sip on her wine.

After a while she asked, "How long does it take to simmer?"

"You that hungry?"

"Not exactly." She looked down at her plate and noticed she'd already plowed through everything but the brie and a couple of the pecans. "Just pacing myself."

"Well, it's really just a chicken and wine stew. But it takes a lot of patience. Once everything's browned and in the pot, it needs to simmer low and slow—about an hour, give or take. That's where the magic happens."

She snorted into her wine glass. "You make it sound so... Food Network." Her nose crinkled. "Sorry."

"No, don't be. I take that as a compliment." His eyebrows lifted. "But it's clear we're going to have to find something to occupy you while I cook. How about Word Trap?"

"No idea what that is," Cali confessed.

Ethan wiped his hands on his apron—another of the many things he brought along with him—and grabbed the bottle of pinot noir to top off her glass. "We agree on a word, and if you or I say that word at any point for the rest of the night, we have to drink."

Cali's eyes grew wide. "The whole glass?!"

Ethan frowned and shook his head. "Hell no. I don't want to be remembered as the guy who came to cook you *coq au vin* only to make you vomit before you even tried it. No," he insisted. "A sip. You must take a nice, healthy sip if you say the word. That's all."

She eyed him skeptically. "What's with you and games? Just like when we were at the fall festival. Now you want to see me beat you at a drinking game, too."

He scoffed. "Okay. Then beat me."

She took a sip of her wine, confident she'd win even though she was already in the lead on drinking tonight. Words were her specialty. Ethan didn't stand a chance.

"Okay, what word?" she asked. "Make it a good one."

Ethan glanced over at Max, curled up on a rocking chair several feet away from them. "How about 'cat'? Neither of us can say the word 'cat' without drinking for it. Deal?"

This … would be tough. Sometimes cats were all Cali could talk about. Especially now that Max was in her life, she could see herself slipping up on this one easily. "It's a challenge," she said. "But deal. I'm still suspicious this is your way of making sure we end up talking about football or something."

He laughed but didn't deny anything. They shook on it, then Ethan meandered to the counter to pour himself a full glass of wine, too. "Okay, Jacobs. Since I picked the word, you get to start. Ask me anything."

Cali bit her lip as she thought. So many places to start. "Tell me about Catsby," she landed on.

Ethan froze mid-stir. "Ah-ha!"

"Nope. Doesn't count," she shot back. "That's a name. Like Max. I can ask about your—" She stopped herself just in time. "—pet."

"Mm hmm." He smirked. "You were *this close* to losing already."

She scoffed. "Fine. Tell me about when you first got ... her."

"You mean *the cat*?" he said deliberately. He lifted his glass to his lips and sipped.

"That's cheating."

"It's hydration," he said, deadpan. "Okay, okay. I promise I'll behave." He cleared his throat. "Well, let's see. She just ... showed up. I wasn't looking for a pet. She was stuck in the rafters of a half-built community home outside of Chicago. Took me, an apprentice, and one very annoyed foreman an hour and a can of tuna to get her down. Foreman said if I was that determined, she was my responsibility. So I took her home, bought her a sparkly collar. And she repaid me with Gatsby-level partying at 3 a.m., curtain-climbing and chaos included."

Cali laughed. "Hence the name. Well, at least the foreman approved. I mean, I've always believed that your cat finds you, not the other way ..." Her voice trailed off. "Shit."

Ethan's mouth twitched, betraying his amusement. Cali took a swig of her wine.

"Anyway, she's the best. She adapts really quickly each time we move. What about you?" Ethan asked. "Any other ... uh ... *felines* before Max?"

"Clever," Cali commended him. "I'll have to remember that one. No, he's not the first." Her stomach dropped a little at the thought of her Charley girl. "My other ... feline had been with me since high school. Her name was Charley. Tabby, with the most beautiful green eyes I'd ever seen. She lived to 16.

CHAPTER 13

Actually, my grandma found her here, in Autumn Ridge, at this house! But she had too many pets of her own. So I drove down, and the minute our eyes met, I knew Charley was going to be mine. My grandma thought so, too." Cali's eyes got a little misty then. "She'd curl up on my arm each night, nose to nose as we fell asleep. My best friend. I still miss her." She walked over to Max and gave him a squeeze, trying to calm the wave of grief before it drowned her.

Ethan's expression softened, the teasing gone from his face. "She found you here, huh? Guess that makes this place even more special. And it sounds like she was lucky," he said quietly, "to find someone who saw her like that."

Cali was on the edge of something. Maybe it was the wine. She didn't plan on getting to know him like this tonight. How was this supposed to be light and fun and flirtatious if she started crying? She was ruining the whole plan. She sat at the high top again and wiped at the edge of her eye.

Ethan was already making his way over to her with a speared, browned mushroom. He blew on it before offering it to her. "Chef needs a second opinion."

She leaned forward, lips brushing the tines as she took it in, some of her red lipstick lingering on the silver. "Perfect," she said. She licked a drop of butter from her lip.

Ethan's eyes flickered for a moment, as if he'd short-circuited. As if he wished he'd been the butter. As if he'd have licked the butter off her lips if she'd just asked him.

"I've been thinking of getting another cat," Cali said offhandedly. "You know, to keep Max company?"

He froze, then dropped his head between his hands. "Cali ..."

"I said it again, didn't I?"

He nodded, and they both burst into laughter. "Drink up,

Jacobs. But not too hard," he advised, his voice softening again. "I'd hate for you to be too dizzy to enjoy the main course." There was something almost devilish about the way he said it. "Your turn to ask me something."

As the meal simmered, they talked and teased in circles—about music, about the town, about how that word *cat* somehow blurted from each of their mouths at least once every ten minutes. Ethan's laughter came easily, rumbling through the narrow kitchen, and Cali's tension loosened every time it did. As the sauce thickened, the lamplight got hazy, the room softened with steam and candlelight, and the scent of thyme and butter curled around them. By the time the timer buzzed, she couldn't tell whether her cheeks were flushed from the wine or from him.

The pot finally settled into a low bubble, so had she, comfortably, beside him at the table. The *coq au vin* was warm and filling and fall-apart tender. The perfect autumn dish.

As he ate, Cali noticed Ethan's tattoo sleeve was a collage of small, interlocking images—a compass, a hammer, several drawings that looked like cats. Not random, she realized now. He lifted his fork as he ate, and her eyes followed the motion, the way his tendons pulled tight, the edge of ink curling just past his elbow. The design shifted as he flexed, and she had the ridiculous urge to reach out and smooth her palm over the lines.

Then she remembered the one she'd seen on his back that first day they both tried to catch Max.

"Tell me about the cat tattoo on your back," she blurted suddenly, cheeks flushed.

The question caught him off guard, as if he hadn't expected her to remember what he looked like half naked. He laughed, low and deep. "That's another sip. You're terrible at this."

She hadn't even realized. "You distracted me," she accused.

He shook his head. "I didn't say a word. Especially not *the* word."

"You didn't have to. The food. The company. I'm officially distracted."

His knees grazed against hers beneath the table, accidentally at first. Then, when she didn't draw hers back, they stayed pressed together. It was as if her whole body leaned toward his without her permission.

"That's a tattoo of Remy, my first cat, before Catsby. He was a runt and scared of everything." Ethan smiled to himself, remembering. "He thought the safest place was on my shoulder, so that's always where he stayed. From the moment I got home, he climbed up there. He even stayed while I cooked."

"Impressive."

"It was more than that. He was like your Charley. Special. One of a kind. He was my *soul* cat."

"What happened to him?"

"He got kidney disease. We tried fluids and a special diet for a while, but eventually that's what took him. Heart-wrenching. Would not recommend it. As if any of us has a choice."

"I'm sorry," she said softly. "I know what that's like, when they're gone but still everywhere you look."

Their eyes met, and something warm flickered between them. All she wanted was for the air in the room to keep buzzing like this—but without the sadness. So she reached for her wine and said, "Okay, new game, please. Time for something lighter before I cry into my *coq au vin*."

"Fair enough," he said. "I have a few ideas." He grinned while dragging his fork through his plate of nearly-eaten *coq au vin.*

Cali bit her lower lip. Ethan rubbed the back of his neck.

"Let's make it a little more interesting," he suggested. "Forget Word Trap. New game: Truth or Kiss."

Before she had a chance to protest, he reached a hand across the table and touched the gray streak above her forehead, twirling it through his fingers. "Tell me about this. Is it dyed that way on purpose or …?" His voice trailed off.

She swallowed hard and tucked some hair behind her ear. She tried to laugh it off with "Oh, that's just trauma." But his closeness and the rising heat, despite open windows, was already making her blush.

"Trauma?" he asked.

"Wait," she said. "Isn't it my turn to ask you a question now?"

"Nope. No vague answers. You can't leave me hanging like that. What do you mean by 'trauma'?"

"Corporate trauma," she said finally, swirling her wine. "You know. Endless deadlines. Too many all-hands meetings and not enough hands to actually help. People getting promoted for surviving the Misery Olympics. Until one morning—poof!—hello, gray hair. That's why I got into library sciences. But I still have the battle scar."

Ethan tilted his head, studying her. "I think it's pretty," he offered. That made her laugh, but something fluttered low in her chest. "Okay. Your turn."

Her mind swirled like the last few velvety sips at the bottom of her wine glass. "Okay. I've got one. Truth or kiss?"

"Truth."

"You told me, at the fall festival, how you got used to not feeling tied down. But you're an adult now. You can make your own choices. What are you running from?" Her eyes narrowed, daring him.

He hesitated, smile fading for just a second. Then his broad shoulders shrugged. "Maybe I've been running from everything that's *not this*." The silence that followed was confusing, electric. He leaned in again and brushed his fingertips along her wrist. "Your turn. Truth or kiss?"

"Truth," she replied, almost defiantly.

"What would your friends say if they knew I'd come over to cook for you tonight?"

She thought of Minka, of the way she'd cheered Cali on, of how this didn't have to mean anything more than what it was in this exact moment—the building heat and tension and messiness to come. Everything she'd fought against. "They'd probably say I finally did something reckless and fun. Not exactly words people associate with me."

"Reckless?"

"Yeah, taking a chance on a guy who'll be gone by the end of the year."

His expression floundered a moment then recovered, a flicker of amusement crossing his face. It was as if her answer confused and intrigued him just as much as his answer had confused and intrigued her.

Touché, Cali thought.

Then she went for it. Hard. "Your turn. When did you first notice me? The story I'm telling myself is you sat outside of Minka's every morning, long before I ever noticed you. You'd sip your coffee, pretend to read a book or scroll your phone, but really you were waiting until I looked your way."

Ethan got up from the table and walked the few steps around to her. For a moment, she thought he'd collect her glass or reach for her plate. But instead, he braced one hand on the table beside her hip, the other at her jaw, and kissed her like he'd been wanting to do that for weeks.

His mouth was warm and tasted faintly of wine, the kiss deliberate, unhurried. Not a way to dodge her question, but a way to answer her.

When he finally pulled back, he stole her plate from the table and walked it to the sink to wash it, as though that kiss hadn't just rearranged the air between them. She felt heady and drunk but not inebriated. More like high on the thought of what could happen next. What might happen. What she wanted to happen.

His rough voice echoed from across the kitchen. "And how many times have you thought about us kissing like that since you *finally* looked my way?"

God, he was good. Ridiculously good. He had her in the palm of his hand. And Cali thought how this teasing, this verbal back-and-forth, this matching of wit might be the hottest foreplay she'd ever experienced.

She didn't answer right away but followed him into the kitchen, the narrow space collapsing what was left of her restraint. His gray eyes turned toward her, lingered on her eyelashes, and traced down to her lips. She found herself close enough to smell his cologne, fingertips dancing along the hem of his shirt, until she felt the band of his jeans.

He caught her wrists and spun her gently until her back pressed against the counter. Then he kissed her—harder this time, deeper, the kind of kiss that left no room for confusion.

She felt his body pressed fully into hers, the want behind every one of his movements. This wasn't polite anymore. This was gravity between them, taking over. She slid a hand around his neck.

CHAPTER 13

Then, with a slow, calculated motion, he reached up and slipped her glasses from her face.

"Can I?" he murmured, setting them safely beside the sink.

The world blurred around her, but he was still in focus.

He lifted her onto the countertop, filling the space between her knees with his body, her skirt caught between them. He slid her toward him and paused there, breathless, as she wrapped her legs around him, pinning him against the counter. Her pulse tripped as he lowered his hands to her ass and gripped. The tension between them was undeniable, the way his erection pressed into her center.

"Ethan," she whimpered into his mouth as their lips brushed together again.

He ran his knuckles softly along the front of her cardigan, and her nipples peaked at his touch. He traced them both with his thumbs, a feeling so impossibly electric it made her back arch up for more. "All these buttons," he teased, forehead pressed against hers. "Do you know how many times I've imagined helping you undo these?" He slipped the first one from its buttonhole with a squeeze of his fingers. She leaned back, her hands propped on the countertop, and watched as he undid the second and third and fourth. Suddenly a rush of cool air hit her abdomen, a reminder of the chilled night making its way in.

He cupped and caressed her breasts in his hands. The only thing between her and his warm touch was a thin, beige bralette. Before her brain could scold her for not anticipating this moment, for not slipping on something a little sexier, Ethan bent down and pulled one of her nipples gently into his mouth, cotton fabric and all. He sucked and savored the feel of her until she moaned, then he moved onto the other breast and did it all over again. The feeling of the wet fabric sent a shock through her that made her toes curl and her head drop back.

"Holy shit," she whispered, in a daze. Could she come from this alone? It had never happened before. But Ethan was already full of surprises. "Please," she begged.

As if he understood what she meant, he pushed the fabric of her bra aside and took one of her breasts into his mouth. "You're so sweet," he said. "I could eat you for dessert."

Her breath caught each time he nipped, playful and wanting. Warmth pooled inside her belly.

He ran his hands along her hips and thighs then, down to the hem of her mustard-colored skirt. He hiked it up to her hips, exposing the lacy, silicone edge of her thigh-highs and a glint of her nude panties. "Jesus, Cali. I could look at you like this for hours."

Both of them breathed hard. The world had gone quiet except for the faint clicks of the ceiling fan and the frazzled sound of their breath trying to catch up. Her pelvis rocked toward him. He ran his hands up and down her tights, caressing along the lacy top bands.

"Please, let me taste you," he whispered, his voice thick and rough. "I need to know if you taste as sweet as you look right now. Is that alright?"

For a heartbeat, she just stared at him. No man had ever asked like that. No presumption, no ego, just desire wrapped in respect. The thought made her ache even more.

"Yes," she said finally, her voice barely a breath. "God, yes."

She leaned back on her elbows as he lifted her skirt hem higher, his gray eyes lingering on every detail. He lowered his head between her legs and met her gaze with his as he parted his mouth. Then she felt the warmth of his tongue run along the fabric of her underwear. Cali's mind turned to putty.

CHAPTER 13

The fingers of one of his hands reached for hers, squeezing gently. He took his time tracing along her skin, noting where she quivered or relaxed, making a mental map of all the places and things he might do to her. Then he pushed aside her panties and found her clit with his tongue, building from light kisses to a deeper, firmer rhythm that almost made her come apart.

"Do you like that?" he paused to ask, and she moaned in response.

She couldn't control the sounds that slipped from her lips or the ache between her thighs wherever he touched. She rocked slowly, carefully, into him as he matched her pace. She'd been so fixated on the rugged parts of him—tattoos, deep voice, chiseled jawline—that she hadn't imagined how deliciously lush and soft his mouth might feel against her folds.

He slid a finger inside her and curled it upward as he licked, drawing a sound from her she didn't even recognize as her own.

"Ethan—I about—I'm going to—" she muttered breathlessly. "Please, Ethan. Please."

He darted the tip of his tongue against her, fast and steady, and stroked his finger until she throbbed. She trembled as the waves broke over her, clutching at his hand, biting back the cry that threatened to escape. Then her body shuddered with a grip of pure pleasure. For a moment she thought she saw stars against the backs of her eyes.

Her breathing still ragged, he lifted her carefully from the counter and carried her to the couch. But he didn't jump on her and finish what they'd started. He buttoned her back up, pulled her close and spooned her, kissing her hair as though he had all the time in the world.

For a long while, neither of them spoke. Her breath steadied. He breathed in the scent of her.

Then, softly, he said, "Tell me something no one else in Autumn Ridge knows about you, Cali."

She almost laughed, except his voice had been too sincere for jokes. "That's a dangerous question."

"Whatever it is, I'll keep it safe."

The room felt suddenly smaller, the weight of her confession rising in her chest. Maybe it was the wine, or the softness of him wrapped around her, but the truth slipped out. "I was engaged once. But we were long distance, and he wasn't exactly faithful. When I found out, we broke it off. And I guess I never really figured out how to let someone all the way in after that."

What are you doing?! her brain scolded. *This isn't fun! This isn't sexy!* Bringing up her ex and the heartbreak he'd caused wasn't exactly fuel for the fire they'd just lit. Ethan's arousal still pressed against the curve of her back, steady and insistent. He wanted more, and God, so did she. But her confession threatened to shift everything.

Ethan's fingers found hers, his thumb tracing lazy circles over her skin. "He sounds like an idiot."

She huffed a quiet laugh, trying not to sound bitter. "Or maybe I was."

"No," he insisted. "You were just wanting someone who'd stay. That doesn't make you an idiot."

Was that the truth, though? If she emotionally invested in Ethan the same way she'd invested in her ex-fiancé, expecting them both to stay, didn't that mean the problem was her? The night had been such a roller coaster already, from the loss of her Charley to Ethan's Remy and now this strangely vulnerable moment for her.

"That's why I can't—Ethan, I can't give you everything. Not when you're leaving. I'm sorry." She sighed into his strong arms. "But I promise you, this has been the most fun night I've had since moving to Autumn Ridge."

Ethan stilled, and the unnerving quiet hung between them for a moment. Then he said, "Okay. We stop here. But for the record?" His lips curved into the faintest smile against her ear. "I'd never regret wanting more of you."

She rolled toward him and tucked her head underneath his chin as he pulled a blanket over them both. "Will you stay?" she asked softly. "Just for tonight, I mean. It's already late and we're together and …"

He answered with a kiss—slow and devastating—then nuzzled his nose into her hair and breathed her in.

Outside, the crickets sang, and somewhere a window shifted. But neither of them noticed. She only counted the steady thrum of his heart until sleep overtook her.

Chapter 14

Cali's phone alarm cried out at six a.m., dragging them both from sleep—her fault for forgetting to silence it on her day off.

"Sorry," she murmured.

The blanket had slipped off between them in the middle of the night, so she curled deeper into the curve of his body to guard against the chilly morning. He brushed a kiss to her shoulder, hoping she wouldn't notice the hard-on pressed against her hip. His body had reacted before his mind caught up.

For a moment her brain burned with the thought of rolling over and sweeping her hand along the tent in his jeans, picking up where they'd left off last night, making him climax. But his lips brushed against her ear and he whispered, "Breakfast?"

She swallowed hard. "But what about your ...?"

"Coffee first. Everything else can wait until things have ... *settled*."

Cali relented with a smile and a stretch. "Well, I've got the usual. Eggs. Bagels and toast. Whatever you'd had in mind."

"Oh, I noticed last night," he reminded her. "You're well stocked. Let's go with eggs. Any style but scrambled. Too easy."

"I'll take an omelet then."

"Two omelets coming right up." He shimmied out from

behind her and made his way to the kitchen, turning the lights to dim. "Oh nice. I thought I saw potatoes in there. How about some home fries, too?"

"Sounds delicious," she said, wiping the sleep from her eyes. "But don't you have to go into work soon?"

"It's okay. I clocked some extra hours last week. Carl owes me. He said I could come in late today."

She wondered when he'd had a chance to text Carl. Probably before he ever knocked on her door. Maybe, somewhere between grabbing the wine and his keys, he'd already hoped he'd be waking up beside her.

Her house soon filled with the smells of melting butter, cheese, and brewing coffee, and the pink of morning blushed the walls. Cali thought *I could get used to this* as she watched Ethan cook. Glimmers of slow Sundays, when they would both be off work, unfolding just like today, dashed through her mind. They could fill themselves and retreat to bed and stay under the covers until they were exhausted. Laundry be damned.

Then that pesky little voice interrupted. *If that was even a possibility.*

Ethan pulled her from her daydream. "I noticed a broken plank on your back deck last night."

Cali turned her gaze toward the large windows facing the lake at the base of the hill. The splintered plank looked like broken bone under tan skin. "Yeah, it's been like that for a while," she confessed. "I drank coffee out there in the mornings when I first moved in. But one day over the summer, I woke to that. I haven't been out there since.

"Yeah, it's kinda dangerous. And a shame," he added. "I'll size it and grab some boards before the weekend and repair it next time I'm over."

A coy smile crossed Cali's face. "I see. Already inviting yourself back for the weekend?"

Ethan smiled back. "If you'll have me. I kind of like it here, with you and Max." A warm gaze passed between them. "Breakfast's ready. Come and get it."

Cali wolfed down half her plate before freezing mid-bite, fork clattering against the dish.

"Something wrong?" Ethan asked.

She swallowed down a chunk of potato without chewing. "Max. Have you seen him this morning? I haven't seen him yet." Panic tightened in her belly. "Max! Maaaax!" she called out.

They split up without a word. Ethan rushed up the stairs to the loft and Cali ran down into the basement. After a few minutes they met again, empty-handed, on the middle floor outside the kitchen.

"Bedroom!" Cali gasped, rushing past him.

He bounded after her when they both halted in the doorway. At first it didn't register—the open gap, the breeze—until her eyes caught on the torn mesh and her stomach dropped. Beyond her bed, the window screen hung crooked, its frame bowed outward as if something had pushed through from inside. A few claw marks scratched the sill where paws must have scrambled for leverage.

"Oh no. No," Cali whispered to herself, "I left the windows open."

Ethan placed a hand on her shoulder. "It's not your fault, Cali."

"But it is!" Her voice trembled under the weight of guilt. The curtains swayed in a breeze that shouldn't have existed.

Ethan watched the panic pull her under, like Alice tumbling

CHAPTER 14

down a rabbit hole. "Let's just focus on finding him. He was a stray before," he said calmly. "He knows what he's doing out there. He'll be fine until we can find him."

"But he doesn't know what he's doing," Cali argued. "He's just a kitten. And he's never been this far out of town. While everyone there might brake for him or offer him a bite, it's a little more ... feral out here." Her brow tensed. "What if a coyote got him?"

Ethan shook his head, refusing to consider that possibility. "Look, the windows were open. We would've heard if he'd been in distress. So let's split up. I'll drive toward town, and you can search around here." He cupped Cali's face, grounding her, pulling her back from the spiral of what-ifs. "We'll find him, Cali. We'll call if either of us spots him. I'll text every chance I get, even if I haven't found him yet."

"Okay," she said. "And The Nine. I'll text them, too. The more eyes we have watching for him the better." Cali had spent so much time rescuing strays. She never imagined she'd lose one again. She covered her face with her hands, willing back the tears of concern and embarrassment. "This is all my fault. I shouldn't have let you stay. I should've closed the windows before we fell asleep. I should've . . ."

Ethan shushed her softly. "Stop blaming yourself. Neither of us could have predicted this." He took her by the chin and lifted her gaze and brushed her tears away with his thumbs. "I promise you we'll find him. Promise. We'll keep searching until we do."

Outside, the first morning birds began to sing—a sound that only made the house feel emptier. He kissed her forehead then marched toward his truck, his breakfast growing cold on the plate he'd left behind.

Cali grabbed her coat, keys, and phone and headed out, too, down toward the lake then up the hill, knocking on all the doors where there was someone to answer. She called Max's name through the tall maples and dormant fields for hours, nervously fingering the cat treats in her coat pocket. Ethan pinged her at regular intervals, just like he'd promised, until he finally had to clock in with the crew. The Nine stayed vigilant, flooding her phone with messages and little bursts of hope as the day stretched on without a single sighting of the Maine Coon kitten.

By sunset, the sky had dimmed to bruised violet, and her mood sank with it. Her feet ached, her throat burned from calling his name, and even with half the town helping, she'd made no progress. When she finally stumbled home, she leaned against the door and let herself cry—for Max, for the empty house, for the guilt that clung like a second skin.

Then her phone buzzed in her pocket.

Ethan, separate from The Nine—*You're not going to believe this, but he's been found.*

Cali's heart leapt into her throat. *Where?* she typed back.

No reply—just a photo. A fuzzy hammock, an orange tabby draped across it, glittery collar glinting in the light.

Catsby.

And below her, turquoise eyes peered up at the camera. Wide, curious, unmistakable.

Max.

The relief hit so hard it hurt.

Chapter 15

Ethan texted her his address, and because it was late and he had plenty of cat food on hand, they agreed to meet up Wednesday after work.

Cali recognized the street from his address, not too many blocks from both City Hall and the library. No wonder he'd become a regular at Minka's café each morning and seemed to know everyone in this small town already. He lived—at least for now—right in the heart of it.

The string of townhomes was quaint and unassuming. Brick and pale blue exteriors. Small front porches. Potted plants. Several of his neighbors had decorated for autumn and Halloween, with large spiders dangling in open windows, ghosts and witches staked into their front lawns. Carved jack-o-lanterns, glowing faintly as the sun began to set, seemed to be a popular thing here, too. But not for Ethan. She easily spotted his house number because his old truck was parked in front of the garage. But nothing else gave away that the unit was occupied, except the shadow of a chubby cat with a curiously curved tail in the second-story window.

She pressed a finger to his doorbell, and he opened it before the sound stopped, as if he'd been waiting there for her. Before she could say a word, he scooped her toward him, a hand pressed into her lower back, and kissed her. He was warm and familiar and a welcome contrast to the cool air and the frustration of the workday. In addition to searching for Max all day yesterday, Cali returned to the library to discover the staff had let the interlibrary loan requests be sent to the wrong branches and had devolved into a little spat over who was in charge of what for the day, which resulted in one of the volunteers quitting after feeling overwhelmed. They'd told her they had things under control, but she found herself losing all of Wednesday to getting the library back on track. It was the worst possible timing, too, given she'd only have Thursday and Friday to regroup around the Banned Books Week displays and scavenger hunt. Things were starting to unravel.

He pulled her into the townhome, and she was met with some unexpected charms. The living room was dressed in books and old records tucked beside a speaker. He had a hand-built coffee table in the center, bearing the inner rings of a tree under its glossy topcoat. Sure, the gray sectional had a standard bachelor pad feel, and the kitchen in back was nothing but a few cabinets, a fridge and an oven pressed against a wall. There wasn't even enough room for a proper dining table. Still, it smelled faintly of wood polish and freshly baked bread.

"Watch out for Kicky Minaj," Ethan warned, pointing at the fuzzy-tailed, giraffe-patterned plush toy at her feet. "If Catsby sees you step on that, she'll hold a grudge. She might even cut you."

Cali chortled. "I'd expect no less from one of the Barbz."

She slipped off her ankle boots and glanced around, expecting to see Max or at least the cat tree from the photo Ethan had sent.

"They're upstairs," Ethan admitted. "Both probably asleep.

Have you had dinner yet?"

She shook her head no, suddenly feeling uncomfortable. "You don't have to—"

"I know. But I want to." He gestured to the sofa. "Sit. I've got leftovers," he said, heading toward the fridge. "*Coq au vin*. The famous one. But this was the trial batch, so it might not be as good. I made some tweaks at your place Monday night. Still, couldn't let something that good go to waste." His eyes flicked toward her. "Guess I'm guilty of that in more ways than one."

Cali felt a swirl of nerves in her stomach, but not over what Ethan had said. She didn't sit and instead stood there, wringing her hands together. The quiet hum of the fridge, the lingering aroma of his leftovers, the little tufts of cat hair along the carpet. It all felt too intimate, too safe, for what she was about to do.

"I think I just want to see Max," she said, voice soft but clipped.

Ethan's smile faltered for the briefest second. He didn't push, but something in his expression shifted. A flicker of recognition that something had changed since the last time he'd touched her. She hadn't leaned into his kiss. She hadn't asked about his place or joked about the mix of décor. It was like someone had dimmed the light in her.

"Sure," he said finally, turning back toward the stove. "Let me just set this down, and I'll grab him. Maybe you'll be hungry after you see he's safe and sound."

He turned the knob on the stovetop down to simmer and disappeared to the second floor. She heard them before she saw them, the faint thump of feet on carpet, the low rumble of a purr.

Then Ethan appeared at the top of the stairs, Max perched on his shoulder like a parrot. Catsby trotted behind them, at

Ethan's heels.

"See? Told you he's fine." Ethan had one of those eye-wrinkling grins on his face again.

Her throat tightened. Max's tail flicked lazily, his body relaxed, content. He didn't even meow when he saw her. He just blinked, slow and trusting, before rubbing his cheek against Ethan's jaw. Catsby circled his legs, wrapping her orange tail along his jeans.

She remembered Ethan's shoulder tattoo and his story about Remy, his *soul* cat. That's when she knew she'd lost him. Not only literally but figuratively. If Max had wanted to return to her house by the lake, he would've shown up there. He knew where it was. But he didn't. Instead, he hiked the few miles over hills and through fields in the dark back to the center of town. He'd searched for Ethan after he'd gone missing, not her. And Ethan was the one who found him. Fair and square. Max had chosen Ethan. And maybe, given her lapse in judgment, Max was better off with him, too.

The thoughts kept hitting her like punches as Ethan passed Max into her hands. She squeaked out a pained "Thank you," but couldn't even look him in the eyes when she said it. She smiled weakly.

Cali's arms felt too tight around him, like she might crush him or drop him if she kept holding on. Her chest ached with every purr. The harder she tried to swallow it down, the more it clawed its way up her throat.

"Cali," Ethan whispered with concern, "what's wrong?"

She felt her mouth, so dry, forming the words before her brain could even register them "You should keep Max." She passed the cat back into Ethan's hands swiftly and stepped back.

"What?" he said, his face in shock.

CHAPTER 15

"For his sake," she added. "They could keep each other company." She gestured awkwardly at Catsby, who was also staring up at her, mouth agape. "Like you'd wanted for her. You know? A sister or brother? That's what you'd said. And—and he'll be safer here. Maybe he won't try to escape again. Oh! And your schedule's more flexible. You took him to the vet when I couldn't."

The more she talked, the more Ethan looked unconvinced and confused. "But you love him. I can see it in everything you've said or done since we met. Nothing else is more important to you than Max."

Max was meowing now, and squirming, begging to be let down. Ethan gently placed him on the floor, and he and Catsby scurried back up the stairs.

"I can live without him," Cali lied. "I've lived without a cat before." Her tone grew cold, insistent. She turned toward the door and started marching.

"Wait," Ethan said, and she stopped in her tracks and turned back toward him. A sudden realization crossed his face, and his mouth turned down at the corners. "You're not just letting him go, are you? You're letting *this* go, too." He gestured between them.

Cali knew exactly what he meant when he said *this*. She felt vulnerable, exposed, like an open wound bleeding out onto his carpet. She had to stop the bleeding.

"Look, Ethan. You're not staying," she suddenly blurted out. "You'll finish this project and be gone, and I can't just …" She inhaled, realizing she may have said too much. "… I just can't do *this* right now. Okay?" She mocked his gesture back to him. "Just let me rip off the band-aids—you and Max—all at once, so I can go lick my wounds."

Ethan's tone was hurt but steady. "So that's it? I'm just some temporary distraction with a toolbox?"

Cali felt flustered. "I didn't mean that—I just —"

Ethan interrupted her. "Yeah. You meant it. But tell me, Cali, where do *my* feelings, *my* wants fit into this story you've sold yourself?" He sighed, exasperated, trying to grasp for calm again. "You have no idea how much I want to stay."

He said it like he meant it, but Cali doubled down. "Wanting and doing are two different things, Ethan." She started for the door and grasped the knob with a trembling hand.

"Cali!" he called after her. She turned back and saw the cats again, watching hesitantly at the top of the stairs. Ethan closed his eyes, exhaling long and slow, then lifted his hands in a small gesture of surrender. "I'm trying here."

She nodded stiffly, stepped into the cool air, and shut the door before she could change her mind.

Chapter 16

Thursday's book club duties hung over Cali's head through the night and all the next day. If she hadn't been the sole person able to keep the library open late for The Nine, she would've canceled and stayed at home with a warm mug of cider instead.

It didn't help that the romance rumor mill was churning through Autumn Ridge. Casual remarks from neighbors and patrons alike started funneling into her ears, about catching her and Ethan at the fall festival together or noticing a truck in her driveway overnight or even that her car was parked at his townhome. All leading up to the inevitable prying question and two-cent opinion.

"So are you and that guy, like, a thing now?"

"Ooh, good for you," followed by a wink.

And the worst: "It's about time you met someone." As if they were engraving her tombstone already!

She knew Autumn Ridge was cozy, but not this cozy. Now that she knew, she was pretty sure she didn't like it.

By the time Minka handed Cali her sandwich and Oat Couture, Cali was ready to call it a night. The caffeine invigorated her just long enough to kick-start another book discussion, but all bets were off when the caffeine wore off.

Ethan didn't show to book club. She figured that was for

the best. The book they'd chosen was *A Man Called Ove* by Frederik Backman, with shades of Ethan filtering through Ove's character. Like his practicality and skepticism, both masking a tenderness. The more The Nine commented, though, the more Cali realized *she* was like Ove. Routine and guarded, experiencing quiet forms of loss. At least she wasn't a grumpy old man. She had that going for her.

But Ethan arrived in time for the Nine Lives Club, making for awkward glances between them when Leo called them the "the inseparables." It was hardly the truth. They'd just spent some time together, Cali would've insisted. That is, if Ethan hadn't blushed and given Leo a death stare, which only egged him on.

"Come on, you two, spill it. I hear there's some chemistry brewing." He winked at them with that obnoxious, dimpled grin. Cali wanted to crawl under her chair.

"Yeah," Freya continued. "A little birdie told me they saw you two together at the fall festival."

"And my café," Minka added. *That traitor.* "The whole town's shipping you two."

Mrs. Ellery interjected. "What's this about shipping? Are you two going on a cruise?"

"Not yet," Lynne chuckled. "Shipping is just a short way of saying relationship. Everybody thinks they'd make a good couple, Mrs. Ellery, that's all."

"I see," Mrs. Ellery said. "I'll have to tell my grand-daughter all bets are off then, Ethan. You know I sent her your photo."

Ethan raised an eyebrow. "When did you take a photo of me, Mrs. E?"

Mrs. E? Cali had never heard anyone call Mrs. Ellery that before. But the casualness didn't seem to register with anyone but her.

CHAPTER 16

"When you were building my gazebo out back," she explained. Cali cocked her head at that, too. When had he had time to build Mrs. Ellery a gazebo? When had she asked him? "Or rather, I took a photo of the gazebo and you just happened to be in it. And then I just happened to send that photo to my granddaughter and then, well …" Her voice trailed off. "Now that I'm explaining, it sounds rather out of line. But it was all innocent when it started, Ethan, I promise. My point being," she cleared her throat, "I'm happy for you two."

Cali gulped, resisting the temptation to explain that she'd given Max to Ethan then basically told him to keep his distance from her. Ethan wasn't confessing to anything just yet either. Good. They were at least on the same page with this one.

But when she turned toward him, he kept staring down at the floor, refusing to meet her gaze. That muscle in his clenched jaw clenched, and he ran his hand through his hair nervously. A tell Cali was starting to pick up on, now that she knew how he moved. She pushed down the ache growing in her chest and leaned forward into the group.

"New topic," she said. "Since book club's done, shall we move onto the Nine Lives Club gala planning?"

Everyone nodded their heads in agreement, Ethan a little more enthusiastically than the rest, relieved the spotlight was finally off him. "Great. Mrs. Ellery, you said you'd drafted a list?"

"Yes, I'll need you all to volunteer for as much as possible. There's the music."

"Oh, I've got that covered," Bastet said, waving a hand. "My cousin plays the accordion."

Everyone's expression tightened except Mrs. Ellery's. "I think, my dear, we'll just go with a pre-recorded playlist, yes?

Keeps it affordable, and we can control the volume. Turn it off when the bidding starts. You know?"

Bastet nodded her head. "Got it. I can do that, too."

Lynne, skeptical, offered to help her, to everyone's relief.

Freya interrupted. "So I was thinking we should have a cat adoption fashion show. It'll be perfect for social media, and we can all get our cats to come with us, all dressed up, too." The Nine knew enough about Freya to know she never parted with her cat. He hung out in the florist's shop and somehow managed not to eat all the pretty plants while she was busy making bouquets. That being said, not everyone's cat was so well-behaved.

"I'm sure Fred would love to join," started Leo. "But I can't guarantee we could get him to stay."

Laughter burst from Lynne's mouth.

"Yeah, Purrcy's a good boy at the café," Minka added, "but I don't know if he'd be such a gentleman around shrimp cocktails and a cash bar. Just like his mom." She sighed. "Maybe next year, Freya. But I'm down for taking photos of our cats to promote the event. If you all send me some of your favorites, I'll make captions. We can even snag a handle or hashtag. Something with 'Nine Lives,' if it's available. I'll make fliers for consistent branding, too."

"Brilliant, Minka," Mrs. Ellery replied, adding it to her list. "That's just the kind of thinking we need to get more people interested quickly. But there's more set-up. Um. Volunteers for lighting, sound, temperature checks?"

Leo raised his hand. "Totally my area."

"Then it's yours, Leo. And I already have Freya down for floral arrangement, Lynne for drinks. So, Tabitha, maybe you could help me decorate?"

CHAPTER 16

"Sounds like fun."

"Then that leaves the fine details of our silent auction." She turned to Cali and Ethan, and Cali's stomach dropped. "I hope I can count on you two to collect, log, and price our silent auction donations since you're—what was it? 'shipped'—anyway?"

On any other day, Cali would've been delighted with the assignment. Spreadsheets and tracking were a natural extension of what she loved to do every day. But when she glanced over at Ethan and caught him glaring down at the carpet again, all she could think to stammer out was "I—I think I can handle that all by myself, can't I?"

Mrs. Ellery frowned. "I think not. We don't have a single donation yet. Yes, we need someone to organize it all for the event, which is perfect for you, Cali. But the other side of that coin is getting the donations in the first place. Now, Ethan, I understand you've been making a lot of connections around town. Your name is on everyone's lips—or will be soon, if you keep offering to build folks like me gazebos. Why not use those connections to drum up auction items? It's the perfect pairing. And, quite frankly, I think it's the only way we're going to land this plane on time."

If there was something that could be said about Ethan Cross, Cali realized now, it's that he wanted to help others. She wasn't sure of the motivation. It just seemed to be a part of him. She watched his face soften at Mrs. Ellery's request and his whole body relax into openness. "Of course." He turned to Cali, met her eyes for only a moment and said, "We'll make it work."

Then he took her nearest hand in his.

A quiet tremor ran through her fingers before she could stop it, and her breath caught. He caressed her fingers until she recalibrated, relaxed under his touch. His eyes lingered between her widened gaze and her lips. Time seemed to stutter—wordless, breathless—before he finally let go.

"What about breakdown? You need help with that, too?" he asked Mrs. Ellery. "Maybe Leo and I—"

"Yeah, let the guys handle that, Mrs. Ellery," Leo chimed in.

"Well thank you, gentlemen. I'll strike that off the list, too. I'm sure the other details can be divided next week. Good start tonight, though. This gives me hope."

The meeting wrapped in a flurry of chatter and scraping chairs. Cali was half-expecting Ethan to linger, waiting for her, wanting to talk. But he didn't.

By the time she locked up, the parking lot was empty except for the faint glow of headlights pushing down Main Street. She couldn't swear it was his truck, but her gut told her it was. She walked to her own car, lonely and dimly lit under the weak yellow of a streetlamp. The echo of laughter still hummed faintly behind her, but the warmth of his hand was already slipping from her skin. A memory cooling in the night air.

Chapter 17

Banned Books Week kicked off with less fanfare than Cali expected. But after a day or two of dedicated marketing by the front desk staff, whispers of the scavenger hunt and questions about the LED pointers circulated the library faster than the books. Cali was relieved the town's focus was finally on something important for a change, not whatever was or wasn't happening between her and Ethan. Just like all small-town gossip, they were already onto the next big (or little) thing.

Still, her mind kept returning to the last book club gathering and how Ethan's hand so effortlessly reached for hers while they talked. Had it been sign of understanding? Like he didn't want to deal with Nine Lives Club drama, so he'd leaned into anything that made it look like they were still into each other? Or had he been reaching out because he hoped there was still a chance between them? And she hadn't done anything but freeze.

He said they'd make it work. But what had he meant? The gala preparations or something more? She wished he'd stayed afterward so she could ask. And each time she thought to text him that question, whatever she typed on her phone sounded so weird when she read it back to herself that she never pressed send.

Even during work, she shook off the temptation to reach for her phone when that question resurfaced. It was better to let it be. What she needed was a distraction. So she kept texting Minka instead, who was full of stories about Purrcy's shenanigans at the café or the latest gossip she'd overheard. Tom the realtor's son had been suspended from school for cursing. The owner of the Round Barn had been asking around about catering services, even though they didn't host events. And there was a rumor everyone was going to meet up at Lynne's bar this Halloween again to celebrate Leo's birthday.

Life seemed back to normal.

Minka even suggested they venture out to Candlewick Orchard over the weekend, something they'd done a few times since Cali moved to Autumn Ridge. It was just the kind of apple picking, maple smelling, farm animal feeding diversion she could sink her teeth into, and suddenly there was something to look forward to again.

Every time someone asked her about Max, she deflected, saying he was "fine" or "great" or "hanging out with his friend Catsby". Eventually everyone moved on from wanting updates, too.

Then Ethan stopped by the library. She caught him unannounced at first, searching through the stacks with his own UV pointer in hand. Then later, while she was hidden in her office, he knocked on the door. He wasn't supposed to look *that* good under fluorescent lights.

"Hope this isn't a bad time," he said. "Russell said you'd be back here."

Cali nodded. "Come on in."

They pulled up seats opposite of each other at her desk. He smelled of sweat and cedar and a hard day's work under the falling leaves. A faint fleck of white paint ran along one of his cheeks. He must've just gotten off work and headed right over.

He reached the arm with the tattoo sleeve into his pocket. "I brought the initial list of auction items I'd secured," Ethan told her, handing her the list. "I wanted to make sure those are the kinds of details you need or if I should be recording something else."

Item names, descriptions, quantities, and fair market values were scrawled across the page.

"This is a really good start," she said. "But I think, if you know them, add the donor contact information, display needs—like props, signs, or special space requirements—and maybe the pick-up or delivery details." She squinted, analyzing. "Oh, and I don't see any on here now, but I expect we'll have donations of tickets or services or experiences. If we do, we should mention if there are any expiration or blackout dates."

She looked up to find Ethan gesturing to the cup of pens on her desk. "Could you, uh, repeat that?"

"No, it's okay. Sorry. I was already drafting up the spreadsheet. Let me just print you a copy with several blank rows. It'll be easier."

"Or how about you just send it in a shared note?" he suggested. "That way you could update it in real time, whenever you got an alert something was added."

"Great ... great," she said. "I'll just message you when I have all the columns finalized. There'll be a few for post-auction tracking. Winning bid. Who won. Thank you note sent. So just ignore those."

God, this sounded so *formal* all of a sudden, like she was talking to an attorney or a teller at the bank instead of the only man in Autumn Ridge who knew what she tasted like under her skirt. Her body shuddered at the memory.

"So what did you think of the scavenger hunt?" she asked, changing the subject.

"Just as fun as expected," he offered.

His smile was unreadable. She wasn't sure if he was being polite or if he just looked tired after a long workday. It looked like he might be trying to gauge her reactions, too, and coming up short.

"That boring, huh?"

He chuckled, and it was like a spark igniting the air in the room. "Not at all. It was very ..." He chose his word carefully. "Educational."

"Well, that's the point, I suppose," she conceded. What on earth was going on here? Something was off. She felt that question gnawing at the back of her throat as Ethan shifted uncomfortably in his chair.

"I hope you don't hate me for this, but ..." *Oh no.* She tried to prepare herself for the next words he uttered. *Carl's got the crew packing up this weekend—earlier than expected.* Or *I'm seeing another woman.* But instead he sheepishly lifted his gray eyes and asked "Can I show you some pictures of Max and Catsby?"

Cali's jaw went slack.

"They're just so cute together, and I can't decide on which photos to send Minka for the gala social media posts. Or maybe you had an even better one of Max?"

Cali's smile was bittersweet. "No, I forgot to take photos. He wasn't with me for that long." She felt a stab of grief in her chest but tried to push through. "Here. Show me."

Ethan ended up showing her over two dozen photos he'd taken since Max showed up at his place, including the one he texted Cali the night Max was found. Together, sharing a

CHAPTER 17

sunbeam then tails entwined while they practiced synchronized loafing. Catsby alone, mid-stretch then making biscuits in her favorite blanket. Max, glaring in judgment at the camera then donning a 'I heard the treat bag' expression.

It was almost too much to bear, so she stopped him, uttering "Scroll back" and pointing randomly at one photo of each.

"These? You sure?"

She nodded. "But I guess all of them are great."

"Okay." He cleared his throat and shrugged his shoulders. "I'll send them to Minka."

The chime of a successfully sent message rang, and for a moment, Cali felt the eerie silence of the library creep between them like a fog, thick and heavy.

Then Bernadette appeared in the hallway, balancing a box of donated books in her hands. When she glanced in Cali's office, she spotted Ethan and stopped. "Ethan! Hey! That cat tower you built is gorgeous. Thank you again."

She smiled and was gone before Ethan could even form a reply.

"I guess Mrs. E—as you called her last week—was right," Cali said. "Word's getting around about your services."

Ethan smiled faintly, like he knew it was time to leave but couldn't quite bring himself to do it. "Guess I'll take that as a good review." He rubbed the paint fleck from his cheek. "You want to be the first one to post? Hashtag Crosstown Repairs— 'For When Things Fall Apart.'"

Cali giggled. "Crosstown. Clever. You'll have to run that by The Nine, though," she joked. "I'm sure they'll have opinions."

"Well, I was going to go with 'Fixing What Needs Fixing— Especially If It's Complicated.' But that's a mouthful and maybe a bigger promise than I can keep."

His cheesy grin was infectious, but she found herself unable to return his smile.

Cali felt bad now, for having made him uncomfortable, for drawing this out to the point he was improvising fake slogans just to fill the gaps in their conversation. This wasn't like him. His confidence waned in front of her, and she hated seeing him this way. Her throat ached with things she couldn't say. That the tower he built Bernadette's cat should've been a tower for Max at *her* place, that she was jealous he was building new memories everywhere she wasn't.

"Anyway," she said, clearing her throat. "You probably need to get going. If Catsby's dinner is late, there's no telling what wrath will befall you."

He hesitated a moment too long, then nodded. "Yeah. Long day. See you at book club later this week?"

"Sure. Take care, Ethan."

When the door closed behind him, the scent of cedar lingered. She turned back to her monitor, but she couldn't focus. She plunked a few more titles on the columns of the auction spreadsheet and queued up a shared note for Ethan. It took him over an hour to reply, and when he did, it was only a thumbs-up emoji.

She stared at the emoji until the phone dimmed in her hand. That was all she was going to get, she guessed.

By the time she made it home and into her comfy pants, she'd already typed the message to Minka:

Hey, could you host The Nine at the café this Thursday? Think I'm coming down with something.

She hit send before she could change her mind. She just knew she couldn't sit through another talk about the gala preparation pretending things were normal.

CHAPTER 17

Minka replied almost immediately. *Oh no! Of course! But I knew this was going to happen. Too much fun during Banned Books Week.*

Cali replied with a laugh emoji.

Let me know before Sunday if you still want to go to Candlewick Orchard. If you're better, I can still get Harlow to cover me at the café.

On Friday, Mrs. Ellery also texted Cali that she'd work front entrance as one of the greeters on gala night and hoped Cali felt better soon.

But no other messages came from Ethan, and she didn't dare send any either. If she didn't reach out, maybe the feelings would fade. They always did, eventually.

She remembered how this whole un-tethering process started with her ex-fiancé. The long gaps in communication, the second guessing, the sleepless nights. If, back then, she'd been able to jump forward in time to see how much better life was *after* him, she would have never wasted so much energy trying to keep him. But that wasn't the lesson that echoed through her brain when her head hit the pillow that night. Instead it was a heady soundtrack of questions only Ethan could answer.

Chapter 18

On Saturday morning, when Cali figured out how to phrase it, she told Minka her illness was in her head, not her body, and she was feeling well enough to go to Candlewick Orchard on Sunday. Minka reiterated the importance of taking breaks, and Cali reminded her Candlewick Orchard would be just that.

The ride to the orchard with Minka lifted Cali's spirits almost instantly. Soft sunlight filtered through the color-changing trees as they rolled along an almost vacant Sunday morning highway. The sunroof of her SUV was open, inviting in the cool breeze.

"You going home for the holidays this year?" Cali asked.

Minka shook her head. "Doubtful. I can't really leave town for the holidays because of the café. So it's a good thing my parents and siblings are still mostly local." She adjusted the visor against the glare. "But we may get a visit from some relatives in Indiana. Cousins and their kiddos. It's been a while since I've seen them. Talking on the phone's just not the same."

Cali was reminded of her own family. They'd mostly stayed put in New England, although no longer at her childhood home. She didn't blame them. There was something about New England autumns that no other place could touch.

"What about you? Any plans?" Minka asked.

"There's no telling which direction I'll be driving for Christmas this year," she replied. "Autumn Ridge is that sweet spot between my brother's place down in Connecticut and my parents' place up in Maine."

The wind whipped through Minka's golden blonde hair. "Maybe they'll all come visit you this year instead. Then they can meet Ethan." She winked.

Cali offered a faint smile before taking a long sip of the Oat Couture Minka brought her for the trip. She wondered how long she could avoid the topic of Ethan but was determined to deflect and distract as much as possible.

Cali's phone buzzed in her lap. A text from her mom: *You seeing anyone? Just wondered with the holidays and all.*

"Speak of the devil," she muttered.

"Your mom?"

Cali nodded.

Minka laughed. "Parental telepathy. Works every time."

"Apparently so." Cali slid the phone face-down. "She's got a sixth sense these days, when I'm talking about them. It's like she knows." But Cali couldn't share what her mother texted. She needed a change of subject—and quick. "Tell me about the family who owns Candlewick again. You say they're the ones who supply your apple cider doughnuts at the café?"

Minka was easily distracted when it came to suppliers. "Oh yeah, for years. Mine and pretty much every other small food business around here. And my apples. But it's fun to go pick some for your own use. Oh, Mr. Winslow brought a new one for me to try this year: Ludacrisp. Can you believe it?" They both snorted, recognizing how similar the name was to a famous rapper. "I'm sure they just named them that because they're ludicrously good. Like, *amazing*," she emphasized. "Tropical even. Like if an apple and a pineapple had a baby."

"That does sound good."

As the miles passed by them, Minka fell into a deep explanation of apple varieties and cross-pollination.

Cali finally had to interrupt. She couldn't stand not knowing. "How do you know so much about apples, Minka? You run a café. You didn't grow up in an orchard."

Minka cheeks turned rosy, and Cali watched her straighten her back against the driver's seat. "Oh, well, Grady Winslow and I, we ... well, I don't know what you'd call it, Cals."

"You dated?"

"More like hooked up. Off and on. Like every summer during college. I don't know why but something about coming home and seeing him, it just ... he's the one who got away."

"That's so sweet, Minka. Maybe you're his one who got away, too."

"Meh," she shrugged. "It wasn't meant to be."

"Will he be there today?" Cali asked.

Minka scoffed. "No. Ever since Candlewick expanded into ciders, he's traveled to food expos and regional fairs. He even went out of state for a while to study sustainable farming after I was done with my business degree. I know he's still part of the family business, but not, like, the face of it."

"I see."

Minka's shoulders relaxed as they followed the handmade signs along the road to a gravel lot packed with vehicles. A kid ran past their parked car with a caramel apple on a stick. The delightful smells of wood smoke and apple cider drifted through Minka's open sunroof as they bundled up. Laughter echoed in the distance.

Once they walked through the ivy-covered entrance gates,

CHAPTER 18

they were met with an irresistible fall setting: rows of apple trees heavy with red, green, and gold fruit, rustic wooden signs pointing toward "Cider Barn," "Donuts," "Hayrides," and "Petting Zoo." Wagons creaked and horses snorted as they pulled groups of apple pickers toward the fields. Boots crunched on gravel as goats and cows bleated for more feed. The sweet, heady scent of ripe apples and cider hit her nose first, and she insisted they eat before apple picking. They sat on glossy red benches, each with a cold, fizzy hard cider and warm, glazed apple cider donuts that left them with sticky fingers as they people-watched. Then they wandered over to the animal farm and bought some feed. The nudge of a goat's nose and the feel of its raspy tongue as it ate from Cali's hand reminded her of autumns with her grandmother, visiting together.

Finally, they bought their baskets and made their way out to the orchard to pick them full. The orchard smelled like cider and damp leaves, the kind of sweetness that could trick a person into thinking the world was uncomplicated. Cali trailed behind Minka, pretending to study the rows of apple trees.

"You're awfully quiet," Minka noted, twisting an apple off its stem. "And don't say it's because you're concentrating. This isn't the library." The sound of fiddles tuning drifted from the barn. "Give it to me, Cals."

Cali shifted her basket, scanning for excuses. "Okay. It's Ethan. But before you say anything—"

Minka's brow rose. "Oh, I'm *definitely* going to say something if it's about Ethan."

Cali sighed, pressing her thumb into the skin of an apple until it dimpled. "We haven't actually been seeing each other. At least not regularly, and certainly not like the rest of Autumn Ridge seems to think."

"But the kiss and the cat sharing and the hand holding at Nine Lives?" Cali winced at the reminder. "I thought things were going great. No wonder you haven't been spilling the details."

"I just don't want to get attached, okay? He's going to leave when City Hall's done, and things will get messy. I'd rather rip the bandage off now than wait until later, when it'll just hurt worse."

Minka leaned her hip against a tree trunk, watching her. "You really think you can schedule heartbreak?"

Cali frowned. "That's not what I'm—"

"It's exactly what you're trying to do." Minka's voice softened. "End things before they can end on their own, like that'll make it easier. Right? Well, take it from me. It doesn't work. You'll just end up hating yourself."

The orchard wind rustled between them, shaking loose a few red leaves.

Cali's throat tightened. "I just—if he does leave, it'll mean I misread everything."

"Or," Minka said gently, "you're a kick-ass librarian who isn't prone to misreading. What you're prone to, instead, is making up stories in your head. You're not scared of him leaving, Cali. You're scared of what it says about you if he does. But I'm here to tell you, if he leaves, it likely has nothing to do with you. Do you see the way that guy looks at you? Hell, even the way he looks at your cat!"

Cali glanced down at the trail and swallowed hard. "I gave him Max," she confessed.

"You *what*?" Minka almost dropped her basket. "Why didn't you tell me this?"

"After Max ran away, he showed up at Ethan's place. I saw how happy he was with Catsby and I just—I just, I don't know.

I let go. I told Ethan I wasn't taking Max back, and we got into an argument about it."

Minka blinked at her, stunned. "Okay, wow. That's ... a lot of feelings wrapped up in one cat."

Cali's voice wavered. "I thought it was the right thing. Max seemed happier there—and safe. He probably won't run away again. But now I don't even know if it was about Max or if it was about trying to prove something to Ethan."

"It sounds an awful lot like you were doing what was safest for *you*."

Cali frowned. "What's that supposed to mean?"

"It means you thought if you let go first, it wouldn't hurt as much when they leave. Both Ethan *and* Max, Cals. I see right through it. You thought it would make you brave." Minka dropped an apple into her basket and sighed. "Trust me, it doesn't. It just makes you lonely."

The sounds of the orchard filled the silence between them then. A bee hovered between them then moved on. A camera shutter clicked as someone captured the perfect shot in the next row of trees. Somewhere, a child laughed near the cider press—a sound too bright for how hollow her chest felt.

Cali's chest ached. "You make it sound like I did something wrong."

"No, Cals. I think you did something *human*." Minka smiled faintly and took one of Cali's frigid hands in hers, so Cali would know Minka was being sincere. "But I've played that game before. Told myself I was being practical, giving someone space so I didn't get hurt. All it really did was make sure he never knew I wanted him to stay." She sighed again, heavy with the memory. "I just don't want you to make the same mistake I did. If you want Ethan to stay, you've got to tell him. Otherwise there's no way he'll have a chance to decide for himself." They walked hand-in-hand for a while, minds circling around their own thoughts. Then Minka's voice softened. "By the way, he didn't show up to Nine Lives either."

"Ethan?"

"Yep. When I texted everyone to meet at the café instead, that you weren't feeling well, he said he forgot he'd made plans."

Cali sighed. "That probably just means he forgot he had plans, Minka."

Minka smirked. "I think he didn't want to be there because you weren't there."

"And here I was trying not to be there because I thought he would."

"Sounds like a perfect match to me."

"Oh, shut up." Cali grinned and kicked at a fallen apple with her boot.

"You might as well talk to Ethan about all this before the whole town starts doing it for you," Minka advised.

"No meddling, Minka. You promised."

"I think you two are meddling quite well all on your own, thank you." Minka plucked another apple, tossed it into Cali's basket, and grinned. "Now stop brooding. You're scaring the produce."

Chapter 19

Cali was surprised at how tired she felt when Minka dropped her off at the A-frame house. It had been a Sunday off. Her brain still buzzed from the cider, low radio on the trip back, and the crisp air as day cooled to evening. Not to mention she had enough apples to last her until the end of the year. She fumbled for the house keys with hands full, unable to wave goodbye to Minka, and mused on what she'd bake with the apples first. Her mind drifted momentarily to the image of Ethan in her kitchen, hovering beside the stovetop in his apron, careful with each stir and sip all on her behalf. Her stomach tightened at the thought. It didn't help that everything that smelled like the outdoors in autumn also smelled like him.

Cali set the bags of apples down on her doormat and noticed a piece of paper taped to the front door. She adjusted her glasses and plucked it from the window. The simple script read *Fixed your deck while you were out. Hope you don't mind.—Ethan, Crosstown Repairs*. A smile traced along her lips. Two thoughts consumed her, the first being gratefulness. Ethan had promised to swing back by her place and repair the broken plank, and he'd delivered despite everything. Cali wasn't so sure she would've done the same for him. At the same time, her heart hollowed at the thought she missed being home when he swung by. She wasn't quite sure how she would've responded even if she'd been home, but then she knew. After some awkward conversation and maneuvering, she probably would've excused herself, gone to get groceries or gas or just circle back roads around the lake trying to hide from the gravity this man held in her presence. Ethan probably knew this, too, and chose his timing wisely.

But how could he have known she would be at the orchard today? Maybe Minka let the update slip out when she saw him at the café late in the week. Either way, a fixed deck was a fixed deck, and it warmed her to think Ethan Cross had driven back here to fix it.

She traced her thumb over the words "Crosstown Repairs" and laughed softly to herself. One more quip for the growing list of inside jokes they shared. But it was a bittersweet thought. In a few months, would that list be a memory of him, or would he hang around Autumn Ridge so they could keep adding to it? She thought of Max then, too, his soft fur beneath her fingertips. The house had ached with emptiness ever since he'd run off. She didn't know which of those two she missed more.

Minka was right. Cali knew she was right. If she wanted Ethan to stay, she had to ask him, stop making him try to read her mind. But her head kept resisting the hope that pumped blood through her veins, that he'd stay and somehow this would all work out. Him and Max both. A part of her still thought she was dreaming.

She folded the piece of paper and stuffed it in her pocket then entered the A-frame and set the apple bags on the countertop. Beyond the sliding glass doors, the deck was bathed in the glow of a soft, red sunlight, water glistening from the lake beyond it and a few breeze-kissed trees framing the view. The image pulled her toward it until she found herself on the back deck, smoothness underfoot, the faint smell of sawdust and fresh wood stain still carried in the air. His craftsmanship was perfect. The size. The cut. The color of the stain. Despite the age difference of the planks, it looked as if that break had never happened. She wondered then if he'd replaced more than one board or had somehow weathered the stain to match the rest of the deck. Whatever he'd done, it was beautiful.

She rushed back inside, and before daylight completely disappeared, she made a cup of chamomile tea and pulled out the old papasan rocking chair from the garage—the one that sat out there before the deck was compromised. One deep inhale and a sip, and she found herself curled into a flannel blanket, body pressed into the overstuffed chair cushion. It was heaven. Pure heaven. She'd missed this so much, too. She stayed there, rocking softly with her mug in hand until the sun extinguished behind the lake, leaving bands of gold and pink painted across the sky as it melted down.

Once her mug was empty and her pulse calmed, she pulled her phone out of her pocket and found the abandoned string of texts between her and Ethan from before. She typed out *Thanks. Deck looks great.* a few times only to erase it again. When she read it back to herself, she was unsure how that made her sound. Too cold? Too succinct? In the end she decided to send the message anyway but included an actual photo of the deck and comfy chair, her mug peeking from the corner of the frame and the last of the daylight a backdrop. She expected him to take a while to reply or to not reply at all. But within minutes, her phone was vibrating on her lap.

Ethan—*That view deserves a brochure.*

Cali—*I'd rather enjoy it than advertise it.*

Ethan—*You got two of those chairs?*

Cali—*Just one. You snooze, you lose.*

She watched as three dots appeared and disappeared, the seconds ticking by. She grabbed the blanket, trying not to fixate on what he'd reply next, and retreated into the warmth of the house. Finally he messaged *I'm just glad you're safe.*

She didn't know where to take it from there. She typed out every thought that entered her head, like *It's all because of you* and *Are you free right now?* But nothing seemed to fit the moment. She found herself deleting all of them except *I made a mistake*, which she accidentally sent. Her heart raced in her chest as she scrambled for an excuse.

On the spreadsheet. Sorry. Pressed send before I was ready. Can we meet up at the library a couple days before the gala to cross-check what I captured?

It was a long shot, but Ethan's reply seemed to imply he knew what was in her head. *Sure. Let's do Thursday. I have to work late Friday.*

Her interest was piqued. *City Hall stuff?*

No. Side gig.

That was all he offered, and Cali tried not to read anything more into it. But it was hard. It shouldn't matter what Ethan was doing on his Friday nights and where, but it still made her gut tense to know he already had plans.

Okay, she messaged. *Sounds good. Just enough time to make changes before it gets into the Mayor's hands. You know she's our emcee for the gala, right?*

Yep. Oh, he added, *everyone voted to cancel book club and Nine Lives Thursday night. I hope Minka told you.*

She didn't yet. But that's fine. Makes sense since the gala's on Saturday.

Exactly, he replied.

Then after a moment she sent, *Goodnight, Ethan.*

Night, Cali. Don't stay out too long, okay? Nights like this chill you faster than you think.

I make no promises.

She already missed the steady feeling she had while sitting on the deck, before she'd messaged him. Her fingers ran along the edge of Ethan's note in her pocket, and she suddenly remembered the neat, emotionless Post-It her ex-fiancé left when he moved out of their apartment: *Key under plant.* Since he was always traveling, his stuff was barely there to start. But she remembered the finality of the note on her door, the feeling like a balloon deflating. She used to think that about endings, that they all happened at once. A fight, a slammed door, one last word you didn't realize was your last except in hindsight. But her engagement ended like a slow leak, all the love draining out of it, until she stood, note in hand, wondering how they'd gotten there.

She tried to remind herself, as she read Ethan's note over and over again, that the two weren't the same. The notes or the men or even how they'd treated her.

Cali slipped into pajamas, set her alarm for the next day, and sent Minka one last message to say how much she'd enjoyed Candlewick Orchard.

Then her phone buzzed again on the nightstand. A late message from Ethan.

Forgot to mention. That view's missing something.

What's that? she messaged back.

Someone to share it with.

A photo followed—Ethan with Max's fuzzy gray face pressed against his cheek. Cali's heart fluttered, unsure if Ethan meant the *someone* was him or Max or both of them. She stared at the screen long after the glow faded, smiling despite herself.

Chapter 20

By Thursday, Cali's inner saboteur was screaming at her again. She hadn't seen or received a message from Ethan for several days. Every time she thought she might text him, she talked herself out of it. He wasn't even sitting at the café in the mornings anymore. Cali didn't want to admit it, but she'd been sneaking glances across the street when she arrived and left, hoping to catch him at Minka's and naturally start up a conversation. Her mind raced with assumptions like he was trying to avoid her. Maybe he woke up and realized their days would be numbered and avoided his routine at the café so he wouldn't get caught up in her expectations. They couldn't have a conversation about it if they didn't even see each other. That's the way things had worked with her ex-fiancé at least.

She busied herself with library administration as often as she could. Searching through endless spreadsheets of ISBNs and acquisition codes. Responding to emails that multiplied faster than overdue notices. It wasn't that she wasn't busy. More like not as busy as she'd been in the days leading up to and during Banned Books Week. By the end of Banned Books Week, half the town had turned in scavenger hunt cards, and Russell was already talking about making it an annual thing. She glanced over at the stack of completed scavenger hunt sheets on her desk—proof that, for once, everyone in Autumn Ridge was reading the same thing for the right reasons. Even Bernadette admitted it was the busiest she'd seen the library since the power outage of 2019. And this time, everyone left smiling instead of complaining about all the food that spoiled in their refrigerators.

Cali was shutting down her computer when someone knocked on her office door late Thursday. Ethan stood there, juggling a stack of books under one arm and a manila folder under the other. She glanced at the clock on the wall. Only a few minutes until six, when they closed. Her mind secretly affirmed this was a sign Ethan was trying to minimize contact with her, but she opened the door anyway.

"Hey," she said halfheartedly.

"Hope I'm not too late," he said, holding up the pile. "Figured I should square up before the gala, both the spreadsheet and my fines."

Cali cleared her throat. "I didn't realize the return desk was still open," she said, eyeing the pile.

"Oh, Bernadette said she'd take care of them. To just leave them outside your office. I figured I owed the library a clean slate before the big night."

"Right. A clean slate," she echoed. "How convenient."

Ethan's expression flattened. "Is this a bad time? I thought you'd said you wanted to settle the spreadsheet today."

She tried to hide her frustration. "No, it's fine. I just expected you earlier. Come on in."

Cali pulled two chairs side by side and rebooted her computer, pivoting the screen so it faced them.

Ethan set down the books and folder and rubbed at his neck. He smelled fresh. His hair was still damp, curling slightly at the edges like he'd just stepped out of the shower.

"Looks like something's brewing," Ethan remarked.

He pointed through her open window blinds in the direction of some menacing black clouds. The sky was already getting dark from the onset of dusk. But with the oncoming clouds in the mix, it already looked like the middle of the night out there.

"Then we better make this quick," said Cali, threading the needle she suspected he didn't want to thread. What was the point of even agreeing to come anyway if he actually didn't want to see her? She motioned at the chair, and he sat down to kick-start the cross-comparison of her spreadsheet, the shared note, and some last-minute donations he said he'd secured.

She tried to concentrate on the screen, but the rhythm of his breathing beside her kept stealing her focus. He was so close to her. Had she placed the chairs that close together? One brief reminder of the way his knees touched hers under the table during that dinner at her place almost undid her. Each time he leaned forward to point something out, the clean scent of soap filled her lungs until she forgot which column she was editing.

Three of the items added since they last checked were anonymous donations. Ethan brushed it off, saying any concerns could go through him. He knew the donor. Cali didn't want to argue about how hard it might be to explain that to the mayor, who needed to hype up the donations either by their value or connection to the community, let alone how hard it might be to get answers to follow-up questions after someone won the bid. So she bit her tongue. At least he captured the details she'd originally requested. That was about all they could do for now.

The rain ticked up, a soft percussion against the windowpane. She pretended to read, cross-check and then type, but she could feel the warmth of him in the few inches between them, the faint sound of his sleeve brushing against hers when he shifted documents around in his manila folder.

Ethan, who had been twiddling his thumbs, pulled her from her silent strategizing. "For that porch swing, the donor would like to just provide a few photos. They'll deliver it, but it's too big to bring into the ballroom. Obviously."

She nodded. "Yeah, I was just thinking, if Mrs. Ellery doesn't already have the set-up planned, we might benefit from displaying everything during cocktail hour. Give people time to stew over what they want to bid on. Generate some competition before the competition starts. There's just so much here!"

Cali had to admit the finalized list of donations Ethan secured was extensive. Big ticket items. Small, cherished treasures. Every person in Autumn Ridge had something they could throw their money at. For the first fundraiser the Nine Lives Club ever hosted, Cali couldn't imagine a better assortment. They'd all be fostering strays in no time. She imagined them roaring with enthusiasm once they saw the list.

Ethan blushed. "It's only, like, 30 donations."

"Yeah, well, that's 30 more than we had before," she said. "Did you text The Nine? They'll probably throw a separate celebration in your honor just for this."

The rain began softly tapping against the window, and both of them turned their gaze toward the sound.

He looked at her then, really looked, and for a second she forgot how to breathe. The air between them felt charged—not with tension exactly, but with everything she'd been refusing to admit. She needed to right this, but she couldn't tell if this moment was the moment to try. Her fingers gripped the edge of the paper in her hand.

"You don't have to keep doing that," he said.

CHAPTER 20

"Doing what?"

"Pretending everything's fine when it's obviously not. I'm sorry I showed up late like this. I was so focused on getting those donations. The week kind of got away from me."

His words landed gently, not accusing, and she felt the tightness in her chest ease.

"You're right. I've been ... off," she admitted. "I know. I'm sorry."

He gave a small nod and reached out to her fidgety hand, folding it in his. His thumb traced along her knuckles and the long lines of her fingers. "You don't have to apologize. People pull back when they're scared of losing something. I get it."

Her eyes flicked to his, startled by the truth of it, startled the truth was coming out of his mouth instead of her own. "But how did you ...?"

"Minka told me not to give up on you," he added quietly.

Cali pulled her hand from his and stiffened. "She what?"

"She meant well."

"But I explicitly told her not to meddle in this," Cali huffed. "Why didn't you just come talk to me instead of Minka?"

Ethan leaned back in disbelief. "Every time since—every time I try to talk to you, you've acted like you don't want anything to do with me anymore, Cali." His gray eyes shifted toward the storm and back to her. "How do you think I knew when you'd be away from home long enough to fix your deck? I had to ask Minka. If I'd asked you, you would've told me to forget it."

Cali's jaw dropped. She wanted to argue, to say he was wrong, but the words jammed in her throat.

"Yoo-hoo!" came from the hallway. "Can I borrow Ethan a minute?" Bernadette asked, completely unaware of what she'd walked into.

Ethan couldn't have disappeared from her office faster. *Good*, she thought. *I just wanted to be headed home right now anyway.* She finalized the spreadsheet and emailed everyone who'd need a copy then went to clean out her mug.

Cali rounded the corner just as Bernadette's laughter carried down the hall. She could see the two of them as she washed the mug. Ethan stood with his library card in hand, nodding along. Nothing scandalous, but it still burned like a spark under her ribs.

"Anytime," she finally heard Ethan say. "Have a good night, Bernadette."

Bernadette smiled, waved, and walked out into the drizzle, an umbrella shielding her head. The door slammed once, and Cali expected it to slam again when Ethan left. Suddenly they were back in her office, together.

Ethan cleared his throat. "You okay?"

"Fine."

"You sure? That didn't seem—"

"I said I'm fine." She stacked some paperwork she didn't need to stack, too neatly. "You don't have to charm me, Ethan. I'm not trying to be one of your clients."

That stopped him cold. "I wasn't trying to make you one."

"Then maybe stop treating every woman in this town like she's your next client. Mrs. Ellery's gazebo. Bernadette's cat tower. And God knows what else you've offered to fix."

Ethan blinked, like she'd slapped him. The silence stretched, thick and sharp as the rain starting to drum against the windows. "You really think that's what this is?" he said quietly.

Her voice cracked. "What else could it be?"

Ethan shook his head once, something tight and unreadable flickering in his eyes. "You've had a hell of a way of keeping me guessing, Cali. But this time I'm stumped."

He gathered his folder and his keys, smoothing down his gray shirt like tidying up was the only thing left he could control, and walked out before she could find the words to stop him.

The sound of the door slamming echoed too much like another night long ago—her ex-fiancé leaving after she'd confronted him about cheating, his suitcase half-zipped. The silence then had been thicker than mud, and she'd waded through it alone until dawn. The memory hit hard, heavy, leaving her chest tight.

Fantastic, she thought. *As if I needed that rerun.*

She took a breath, slumped in her chair for 15 minutes, and stared at the ceiling as she listened to the rain. Then she grabbed her purse and got up and turned off the lights and headed for the front door. The rain had turned steady, slicking the streetlights into hazy gold halos. She told herself she didn't care if Ethan was halfway home already. That this was exactly what she wanted—for it to be over, for her not to want anything more from him, for him and Max and the rest of this stupid, stupid year to just fade away.

She turned the key in the lock and stepped into the chill and the rain, shoulders hunched. Then she saw him, leaning against the side of his truck, hands shoved in his pockets. Soaked and stubborn. His head lifted as her heels clicked on her long walk down the ramp. In the distance, thunder rumbled. Maybe he was waiting for her. Maybe not. But she couldn't shake his question *You really think that's what this is?* and the feeling she was about to find out.

Chapter 21

The night air hit her like a wall as she stepped into the drizzle. Figures. Nothing like *déjà* vu and bad weather to make a night complete. Cali quickened her pace toward the lot, the damp scent of asphalt filling her lungs, the word "regret" lingering on the tip of her tongue. Her car was parked not far from Ethan's, but theirs were the only two remaining, the pavement glossed dark by the sprinkles. She tried to pass by him without a word, but he reached out and closed a gentle hand around her arm.

She stopped. "I don't want to talk about it," she said.

"Cali, please," he begged. "What's the 'it' you don't want to talk about? Was it me confiding in Minka? The overdue library books? Is this about Max? I just need to know where to start."

She exhaled long and slow, her breath fogging the air between them. "All of it. And Bernadette," she said. The rain spat against their cheeks.

"But Bernadette paid me," he insisted. "So did Mrs. Ellery. Contrary to what you may think, I'm not flirting with every cat owner in town. The only one I've been flirting with is you."

His hand glided down to her elbow, where he tried to draw her close, but she wasn't having any of it. "Well, I'm not a cat owner anymore, so I don't count," she insisted. She kept glancing over at her car. "Look, Ethan, what you do is your business. I don't care anymore. It doesn't matter. Now can we just both go home before I'm soaked through, too?"

Thunder lit up the clouds off in the distance, a low rumble rolling toward them. Water pooled beneath their feet. A flash of lightning caught his gray eyes, bright enough to burn it into her memory. He licked his lips and shifted under the weight of his soaked clothes and frustration.

"We're gonna get struck by lightning if we stay out here," she warned.

But Ethan wouldn't relent. "You keep saying it doesn't matter, but you wouldn't look at me like that if it didn't."

She closed her eyes, trying to check herself, trying to erase the image of his hair plastered to his forehead and rivulets running down the line of his jaw. Trying to extinguish the small, traitorous flex she felt low in her belly. But it wasn't working.

Finally she said, "The gala's in two days. Can we just act civil until it's over?"

Behind her speckled lenses, she watched his gaze burn at her, steady and determined. "Look, Cali. Max still sleeps by the front door each night, waiting for you. He doesn't even come to bed with me and Catsby. You're all either of us think about."

"You don't have to make me feel better, Ethan. Max chose you. End of story."

"He didn't choose me. He chose *us*," Ethan snapped back. "Why can't you see that?"

The drizzle swelled to a deluge, and her heartbeat quickened to match. Her chest ached from the sight of him, clothes clinging, every contour mapped beneath the wet fabric. Maybe that was the problem. Just being around him felt too close to wanting him. Her anger was the only way she could hide her feelings. Now she was furious *and* soaked, so cold she was trembling. But she was angry at herself.

He stepped closer, close enough for her to see the drops clinging to his lashes. She shuddered, and he pulled her in with his whole body, as if trying to protect her from the storm. Drops hit the pavement in a furious hiss.

He leaned down and whispered in her ear. "Tell me something no one else in Autumn Ridge knows. Tell me you want me to stay."

She bowed her head, her wet curls dripping onto his chest. When she lifted her chin to meet his eyes, he looked *wrecked*—not from pain, but from wanting. His gaze searched her face like it was the only clear thing left in a blurred world. Then nothing—not the downpour, not the cat mishaps, not all the ex-fiancé drama in the world—could stop the words that escaped her lips.

"I do. I want you to stay," she said. "I *really* want you to stay."

A car swished by, forgotten in the blur of everything else. She felt warm and safe pressed against him, the only solid thing left in a world turned liquid. Beads slid from the edge of his collar onto her fingers where they clutched his shirt. It swallowed them, humming, and the world slowed to the space between their mouths, silent and waiting.

Their kiss was tender, almost inaudible at first. Just the whisper of lips, touching between droplets. The rainwater felt cool, mineral, and faintly electric. Then her fingers slipped along his wet skin and clothes and hair, desperate for grip. As the rain pounded against them, she couldn't help but feel like it was washing her fears away.

He turned them around, until her back pressed against the

CHAPTER 21

passenger door of his truck. The kiss deepened, heat curling low as his tongue traced the soft edge of her lower lip, just once, before finding her again. He fumbled at the door latch until it opened. He lifted her into the passenger seat, her fingers still clutching his shoulders. When his palms slid along her thighs, she gasped, reminded of that night in her kitchen. Body pulsing, his lips magnetic, every inch of her skin begging to be touched. He couldn't pull away.

"Get in," she said between labored breaths.

She pushed herself back along the bench seat, suddenly grateful for the extra space—and the lack of a center console—as Ethan climbed into the cabin beside her. The door slammed shut behind him, and all was silent but for precipitation drumming on metal. For a moment they stared at each other, wordless, hair dripping and adrenaline humming. He scooted toward her until they were both in the middle seat, and she climbed onto his lap. His palms found her waist and her lips found his again, their pelvises tilting into each other in a slow, seeking motion in rhythm with the steady beating against the roof. Each time their mouths met it was a spark then a steady burn. The kisses deepened, deliberate and hungry, until all she could taste was him.

"Tell me to stop, Ethan," she gasped, as if swimming toward a finish line.

"I'm trying," he said. But the way he kept holding her told the truth.

He pulled her closer. Her fingers found his belt. Every slow grind drew a ragged sound from his throat, and she wanted to keep pulling that sound from him until she forgot her own name. His shirt rode up, and they wrestled it off between kisses, flinging it somewhere near the floorboard. He kissed down her neck, fumbled with her buttons, until her shirt fell from her shoulders. The air was growing thick and hot, fogging the windows around them.

She ran her fingertips along his pecs and erect nipples, slowly tracing down to his abdomen as they kissed. His body betrayed itself to her touch for a moment, bucking softly underneath her.

"Jesus, Cali," he whispered. "If you keep doing that, I don't know how much longer I can ..."

He looked at her as if whatever she did next could make or break him. He wanted to memorize this, not because he could have her, but because she was letting him.

"I need you inside of me," she said, biting back the words *Even if I regret it tomorrow*. She guided his tongue into her mouth and unlatched his belt. "Do you have—?" she asked hesitantly.

He reached across her to grab his wallet from the glovebox and pulled out a condom. The crinkle of the wrapper cut through the torrent outside. One hand still gripped her firmly from behind. The other dipped beneath her skirt, pulled down his zipper, and slipped on the condom. She bit her lower lip and rolled her hips, slow but full of ache. The length of his cock tented the fabric of her skirt, still draped between them, and brushed against her skin.

"You're so beautiful, Cali," he murmured, and it threw her off balance. How could he still look at her like that—soaked, glasses fogged, hair a tangled mess—with that kind of hunger? She'd wanted to rush this, to lose herself fast before her brain caught up. But the way he held her, the way his hands framed her hips like he couldn't help himself, made her want to slow down and feel every second.

Somewhere in the cabin, a phone rang, too loud, shattering

the moment.

Cali whispered, "Please. Don't stop."

He dug into his back pocket to silence the phone but pressed "Accept" by accident. Unaware, they kissed again and again, Cali's skin tingling with want. She rose, on the verge of taking him in her grasp and guiding him inside of her, when they heard a muffled voice.

"Cross?" They both froze. It was Leo. "You there, man? What's that noise?"

Cali mouthed *Shit!*, her eyes growing wide.

Ethan stammered in shock. "Uh, yeah. Yeah, I'm here," he said. He mouthed *I'm sorry* back at her and pulled the phone from his back pocket. "It's probably, uh, this rain." He cleared his throat and combed through his hair. "The reception—or something. What do you need, man?" She could tell he was trying to hold back the frustration in his voice. He changed the phone's mode to speaker.

"We're at the hotel, getting ready for the weekend," Leo explained. "Something's sparking near the sound booth. If it blows, they'll have to shut down the ballroom. Just thought you might be off work by now. Can you come troubleshoot?"

A muscle along Ethan's jaw tweaked as his face flushed red.

Cali sat back, heartbeat still pounding. "You should go," she whispered.

Ethan hesitated, touching her cheek.

"What's that, man?" Leo asked. "Can barely hear you."

Cali looked away, and after a long pause Ethan said, "Sure. I'll head over."

He hung up, and Cali tried to slip toward the window, but Ethan grabbed her gently by the hips. "I don't have to go right now," he insisted. "I can tell him I got caught up. Either they'll figure it out or the problem will still be there when I get there." His eyes softened at the edges. "Please, Cali. You're the most important thing right now. Tell me what I need to do to make this right."

She wiggled out of his grasp and pulled down her skirt and settled into the passenger seat, arms crossed. She was on the verge of tears, so she kept her eyes fixed on the stream pummeling the truck window. "Can I just stay here a minute?" she asked softly. "I need ..." She shook her head. "I don't know what I need."

"Sure," he said. But his expression turned to confusion. "Do you want me to stay with you?"

"No. I want you to go. Help Leo. I don't know what I was thinking. It wasn't my intent to hate-fuck you in your car tonight, Ethan. I just—" she sighed. "I don't know what came over me."

"But that's not—this wasn't—that's not what happened here, Cali."

She knew he was looking at her then, waiting, expecting her to turn toward him and say something. But she couldn't. He stopped trying to make sense of it. The muscles in his jaw were clenched so tight they threatened to snap. He wrung his hands in his lap then kept brushing back the wet bands of hair that fell in his eyes. Eventually he composed himself and zipped closed his jeans again.

"Okay," he said, voice low, his hand hovering near the door handle. "I don't know what I was thinking either. Seemed like, for just a second there, you forgot what you were running from. See you at the gala, Cali."

He opened the door, rain rushing in again, and slammed it shut behind him.

CHAPTER 21

In the rear view mirror, she watched him jog through the downpour to the back of the truck, grab a clean shirt, and tug it over his bare shoulders. The fabric clung to him instantly. Water streamed down his chest. He didn't even seem to feel it. His expression had locked into something she couldn't read, as he turned toward Main Street and glanced both directions. Under the hazy lamplight, he crossed the road and headed toward the hotel.

Chapter 22

Much to Cali's dismay, everyone in Autumn Ridge except her seemed to be enjoying their Friday morning. She woke to clear skies, the storm gone and the weather even cooler than before in its wake. One of her neighbors was feeding the wild turkeys. Out on the lake, two people fished from a canoe in their down vests and mittens.

Her soaked clothes from the night before still hung by her bedroom door, smelling faintly of rain and Ethan. Of soap and aftershave. Her glasses still had a fingerprint smudge, an echo of what had happened between them last. No, what had *almost* happened between them. It made her head ache. She wished someone had already dressed her for work and made her coffee and told her everything was going to be okay today. Instead, she'd have to do it for herself, and she was sure she could do most of it. Just not that last part.

She checked her phone as she scooped the coffee grinds and the machine sputtered to life. Since she'd sent along the spreadsheet of auction items, there'd been a lot of chattering via email. Lynne, being a bartender, kicked it off around 3 a.m., and as the morning progressed their updates about each piece of the gala preparation got cheerier.

But nothing from Ethan. No private text. No group chat

CHAPTER 22

message. No word from Leo about whether Ethan had saved the gala's sound system or not—and the event along with it. But she was sure he had.

Then Minka picked today, of all days, to use Max and Catsby as the featured felines on her socials advertising the gala. The post appeared while Cali sipped her coffee on her porch. In the photo, the two lounged side by side on stacks of books, likely in Ethan's bedroom or another room she hadn't seen upstairs, with a gala flier nearby. Fairy lights were a blurred glowed above them. "Save the Date" with Saturday's event details were stamped onto the post. She read the description: *Looks like even our mascots found their purrfect match before Saturday's gala. Join us for an evening of saving the strays—maybe your own happily ever after with one of our firefighters! What (or who) will you be bidding on? #AutumnRidgeGala #CatsofAutumnRidge #PawsandProsecco #SaveTheDate #DateNightForACause*

This should be exciting. If things went well, The Nine were about to get a windfall of money for their cause and maybe even a following for their before-unknown gang of local cat protectors. But Cali's stomach dropped mid-scroll, as the comments started pouring in.

AutumnRidgeMayorOfficial: *Can't wait to see everyone there! My wife's been talking about this for weeks!*

ChiefBobisonFire: *Careful, ladies. The boys are already getting competitive over those auction bids. ;)*

SandyBaker799: *@ChiefBobisonFire Is Leo March one of those firefighter dates up for auction? Asking for a friend.*

LeoM_27: *Oh, you know it. @SandyBaker799*

LilaJDesigns: *This post just made my whole morning. Love seeing our town come alive again!*

She couldn't take it anymore, the anticipation that every

vibration, every sound her phone made was going to be a message from Ethan. He said he'd see her at the gala. That was that. She muted her phone, went back inside, buried it in her purse, and dumped the rest of her lukewarm coffee in the sink.

At work she kept quiet in her office for as long as possible, nursing another mug of coffee brewed in the break room. But Russell insisted on asking her a million questions about the gala. What should he wear? He brought her two suits and asked her to choose between them, arguing the other suit each time she landed on a reason for one. Was there assigned seating? Would she make sure he was seated near the firemen that were being auctioned off for dates? Did everyone need to bring their pets?

"Russell," she finally snapped. "I'm just trying to get through one more day of work. Could you please try to do the same? That returns desk pile is about to devour one of our senior volunteers." They glanced over at the poor elderly woman surrounded by books.

Russell was gracious. "Fair enough. I'll save the senior. But if it's an open bar and I go past my limit and start auctioning myself off, you're responsible. Capeesh?"

Cali rolled her eyes. "Open bar. Limit two tickets per guest. If I see you bribing anyone for their tickets, I'll let everyone know *you're* the problem. Capeesh?"

"So sassy," he said. "This is why I love you."

Then he disappeared down the hall.

Near closing time at the library, Minka messaged Cali. *You alive? Haven't heard from you since Candlewick.*

Cali's reply was brief. *Yep. Long week.* She muted her phone again. But the vibrations came quick.

Hey, I've been thinking about what I said to Ethan. I realize I might've stepped in where I shouldn't have.

My heart was in the right place, but I overstepped. No excuses. I didn't mean to make things harder for you two. I shed some tears over this, though, if you want to add them to that enemies vial in your purse...

Anyway, no pressure to reply. Just wanted you to know I care about you both. I'm rooting for things to land how you want them to.

Cali unmuted her phone and texted back. A peace offering, even laden with emojis, was something. *It's okay. I'll collect your tears when you come pick me up for the gala on Friday. I could use a plus one.*

Deal! Minka replied. *Pick you up at 6:30. Be ready for a selfie.*

Cali was relieved at least one thing had gone in her favor today. She hadn't purposefully frozen out Minka. There was enough to distract them all this week. But she appreciated the apology.

By twilight, Cali's house was on its way to smelling faintly of apples and lemon cleaner instead of rain. She had to keep herself busy long enough to reach exhaustion. Only a day and a gala to get through before she could let this thing between her and Ethan breathe or let it go entirely. She couldn't keep falling into his arms every time she convinced herself she was fine without him. So she cleaned the kitchen top to bottom then decided to bake an apple pie with the apples from Candlewick. Her grandmother's recipe called for splashes of lemon juice and cider, thickened with a cornstarch slurry. It was nothing if not a distraction. Better than sitting in front of the television with a bowl of popcorn, though. *Practical Magic* dominated the streaming services this year, and it always made her cry. She wasn't a fan of horror either, but even the one zombie movie she liked was more romantic comedy than horror.

She lugged herself, groggy-eyed and full of warm pie, toward the bedroom when she remembered she hadn't chosen a dress for the event. Her handmade skirts and tops wouldn't cut it this time. She needed something fancier, more chic. So she rummaged her grandmother's things until she found a timeless dress that whispered old-Hollywood elegance. She couldn't believe her luck. A black satin slip dress with a cowl neckline. In the same garment bag, tucked in a pocket, she found a delicate gold chain with a single teardrop pendant. When she put them on, the dress fit like a glove and the necklace fell to the perfect length. Perhaps suspiciously perfect. She looked at herself in the mirror from the front and side and over her shoulder. Even without makeup, she felt stunning.

"I guess we're doing this," she whispered at the mirror. "Thanks, Grandma. Now *two* things went in my favor today. Glad we're calling it a night."

She disrobed and carefully hung the dress and necklace in her closet and zipped up the garment bag. In bed, she piled up her pillows and tucked her feet under layers of cozy until the bed felt like the biggest hug she'd had all year. She turned to her phone on the nightstand and read the rest of the comments on Minka's post then flipped back to her contacts until she found Ethan's name. She reread his text from nearly a week ago—*Don't stay out too long, okay? Nights like this chill you faster than you think.*—and wondered if maybe he'd meant more by it than the weather.

Chapter 23

As Cali waited for Minka to take her to the Inn, she applied one of her favorite, velvety red lipsticks in the mirror. Then she stood back and ran her hands along her hips and the smoothness of the dress, admiring its construction. Both the library's and her old corporate dress codes had been all about covering up. That's why she'd leaned into making her own clothes in her mid-twenties. Department stores didn't sell her style anymore. She could control everything from the fabric to the fit to the color of the buttons, and every piece gave her joy and body confidence.

Now she was wearing her grandmother's old knock-out. She knew she looked amazing, but it was a difficult thought to digest. A part of her felt uncomfortable with so much skin exposed along her shoulders and collarbone. Not to mention the slit that climbed to her knee on the right side. Her mind toyed with the idea of putting it back in the closet and picking another outfit like a cat playing with a ball of twine.

Minka's front headlights pierced the bedroom window, and Cali realized she'd just have to play this off like she was confident. She slipped into some strappy heels that added another few inches to her frame and grabbed for her coat—another of her grandma's well-preserved favorites that she'd never had a chance to wear before. A vintage-inspired red wool coat, richly patterned with tonal swirls and finished with broad lapels and fabric-covered buttons. Prince seams accentuated the waist. It was a timeless silhouette and matched the dress's elegance effortlessly.

A knock sounded, and Cali clamored to the door, coat draped over her shoulder.

"Give me a minute to grab my purse. You need anything? Water?"

Minka stood under the floodlight, her mouth agape and eyes bright and wide as they ran down Cali's satin-draped figure.

"Damn, Cals," Minka said. "Forget the firefighters. They should be auctioning off a date with you tonight."

Cali blushed. "It's too much, isn't it?"

"More like too little—for what people normally see you in," she clarified. "But it's giving me *life*."

Cali covered her chest with her hands and pinched the teardrop pendant between two fingers. "Shit. Give me a minute to change. I knew this was a bad idea."

"No!" Minka demanded, grabbing her by the arm. "Please, look. I need to see you happy tonight. Okay? And if happy means having literally every available guy in Autumn Ridge asking if you'd like another cocktail, then so be it."

"But you don't understand, Minka. You're like the Taylor Swift to my... my ..." her voice trailed off in thought.

Minka raised an eyebrow. "Travis? You're my Travis Kelce? That doesn't compute, Cals."

"No, I'm just, well, anyone shorter and not as model-esque as Taylor. Which I get is, like, most of the world. But my point is to say *you* would look great in this, Minka. *You* would feel comfortable. This is just me being so distracted with Banned

Books Week and the gala prep that I was rummaging through my grandmother's old clothes last night at midnight. I didn't think it through. This dress is not really," she sighed, desperate to make herself clear, "me."

Minka blinked twice. "Well, Cals, you know what Taylor Swift would tell you in a moment like this?"

She thought. "Shake it off?" she winced.

Minka placed a hand on her shoulder. "Exactly. Now get your smoking hot ass into my car, and let's go burn this gala down."

"But first, my purse," Cali reminded her. She ran back to grab it, and they were off.

She was thankful for her coat as they walked toward the Old Ridge Inn's front entrance in the biting evening. But it was heavier than Cali expected, the rich brocade brushing against her arms with every step. She tugged it a little closer as the October chill pressed in then loosened her grasp as the warmth of the grand hotel swept over her at the threshold. A doorman greeted them immediately and sent for a bellhop to escort them back to the ballroom.

The Old Ridge Inn was more glamorous than Cali expected. She'd driven by the historic hotel several times before, but she'd never had cause to stay there, let alone to see inside of the ballroom. The inn seemed to inhale with them as they paused to open the large wooden doors at the ballroom entrance.

"Wow," Minka murmured. "Mrs. E's friend did us a solid."

Crystal chandeliers shimmered above the ballroom, scattering slow-moving stars across marble floors. Velvet drapes framed tall windows, their folds catching the whisper of a night breeze that stirred the candle flames. Cinnamon, champagne, and the faintest note of roasted brie perfumed the air.

Closer to the stage, long tables displayed the town's generosity under soft beams of light. Wicker baskets brimmed with gift cards, Freya's floral displays, handblown ornaments with ribbon bows, and pottery still carrying the scent of clay and glaze. Each item bore a small handwritten card, looping cursive announcing its donor and the starting bid. Even the cheapest bid was dressed like an act of love.

Music drifted faintly from the sound check momentarily then paused, and Cali heard glasses clink together in a far corner. The only other sounds were the soft clicks of waiters' shoes, the flutter of linen being smoothed, and a server counting canapés beyond the doors. Beyond the windows, the town's single clock tower chimed a quarter past six.

It wasn't just pure small-town magic. It was about to be a money-maker. Cali tried to hold back a squeal of delight.

"Ladies," Mrs. Ellery said, materializing beside them. "Come in. Come in." Minka shut the doors behind them. "What do you think? Did Tabitha and I—and our friends at the Inn, of course—pull it off?"

"My brain just shut down from the sight of it," Minka admitted. "Amazing work, Mrs. E."

"Marvelous. Let's put your coats away, yes? The doors will open to the public in fifteen minutes. This way, Cali."

Cali followed Mrs. Ellery to the coat room and listened to some brief instructions for checking guests coats and collecting their general admission fee, as well as reminders about the open bar tickets, food, and entertainment. She told Cali to text her if she ran into other questions before the auction started. Mrs. Ellery promised to have her phone on vibrate all night just in case.

"Now you'll be managing the door with Ethan, so—"

"Ethan?" Cali's tone made Mrs. Ellery's expression tighten.

CHAPTER 23

"Yes, Ethan. Now he's already listened to my lecture about the process. But he's still mingling out there with some of the donors. If he's not back over here in five minutes, I'll need you to go and find him."

Cali felt a lump growing in her throat. "But I thought Minka and I were at coat check tonight. That's why I caught a ride with her."

Mrs. Ellery looked truly perplexed now. "Didn't Minka tell you she and Ethan traded? I swear the cats communicate better than us humans do sometimes." She tsked under her breath. "We needed Minka to take photographs, continue the social media craze she started. Ethan was assigned to carrying in auction items, which is obviously done, and breakdown with Leo, but Rosita said the hotel staff will do that. So he's free to help you."

One of the waiters called to Mrs. Ellery from just outside the kitchen, a concerned look on his face. "You have my number," she reminded Cali, then she turned and strutted off.

Then Cali spotted Ethan from across the ballroom, framed by chandelier light that caught in his wavy, dark hair. The clean lines of his gray jacket—of course he'd wear gray—pulled across his shoulders just so. His dark tie was a quiet arrow drawing her eyes to the steady line of his chest. But it wasn't the suit that stopped her. It was him. The way he carried himself. That irritating, enviable self-confidence and ease he exuded.

Her breath hitched before she could stop it. She told herself it was the warmth of the hotel ballroom, her wool coat, the candlelight. But when his gaze finally swept across the crowd and found hers, the excuses burned away.

It felt like he'd reached for her without moving an inch.

He was mid-conversation with one of the town council

members when their eyes met. For a second it appeared like he forgot whatever point he'd been making. His words caught mid-sentence—enough that the councilman gave him a curious look. Ethan mouthed some excuse she couldn't make out, then stepped away from the councilman.

By the time he reached her side, her pulse was thrumming.

"Cali," he said. "You look ... " His eyes lingered on her hair and traced down the buttons of the coat to her heels then back up to her face. "Stunning. Can I take your coat?"

"I, uh ..." She stared at him, fingers reluctant to let go, as if some part of her needed the armor.

"Practice makes perfect," he said with a disarming smile. "First time taking coats."

She cleared her throat and slipped the wool piece from her shoulders. The fabric whispered as it fell away, gold-threaded red against black satin.

"Oh, this, too," she said, handing him her purse.

The way he stared at her then almost made her want to take off the dress, too. She smoothed the neckline of her gown and centered the pendant, willing her pulse to settle. By the time she looked up, Ethan had disappeared into the coatroom and returned with a ticket she suddenly had nowhere to keep.

"It's okay. I'll hold onto it for you. It's not like anyone's going to forget that coat."

She could almost hear him thinking the words *Or that dress*. He dragged a finger along his jaw, the way he always did when he was trying not to stare.

Leo came through the front doors then, dressed in a blue blazer and pants. His black hair was sharply parted, faded on one side with a long, modern comb-over that brushed against his lashes.

CHAPTER 23

"Well if it isn't the man of the hour," Ethan teased. "You look like you're ready to make some money."

"Or cause a fight," Cali chuckled.

Leo did a double take at her. "Holy shit, Cali. I barely recognized you."

Cali blushed. "Is that a bad thing?"

"No," Leo said. "You look …" His gaze flitted to Ethan for a moment.

"Amazing. She looks amazing, doesn't she?" Ethan said.

Leo just gave a low whistle and gestured his hands as if his mind had blown up. Then he asked if they'd seen Lynne.

"She's manning the open bar they set up," Ethan said, gesturing toward the opposite end of the ballroom. "Arrived hours ago."

"Right, right, right," Leo whispered, still searching the room for Lynne. "Well, I think I'll go see what she's up to before Chief Bob pulls us up on stage. Catch you later." Then he turned his head toward them again. "Oh, and Ethan, no bidding on me tonight, man. Okay? I know you're obsessed. But can we just focus on the strays for once?" His dark eyes glistened.

Ethan chortled and lifted his hands in surrender. "Promise I'll behave."

Leo winked at them both and disappeared toward the bar.

Once he was out of earshot, Ethan leaned toward Cali and whispered, "Okay, I was sworn to not tell anyone this. But you're not just anyone." He inhaled sharply. "Leo's got it *bad* for Lynne."

Cali's skin tingled at the feel of his breath against it, but she shrugged off his comment. "Everyone in Autumn Ridge knows that. But did you *also* know that Lynne and Leo's older brother were high school sweethearts?"

Ethan's eyes grew wide. "No. Leo failed to mention that little detail during our fishing trip."

"And," Cali added. "Lynne used to babysit Leo."

Minka rushed up toward them then with her phone positioned in front of her face. "Say cheese, guys! This one's going live in five."

"Video or photo?" Ethan asked.

"Just photos for now. I'll do video later. But I'll give you a warning."

Cali and Ethan stood a foot from each other, Cali's hands folded across her chest. They both smiled, but Minka frowned at them. "Closer," she instructed from behind the phone. Cali shifted toward Ethan, but not too close. "Closer," Minka repeated. Ethan shifted toward her until his suit grazed her bare skin and covered it in goosebumps. "Now turn toward each other," Minka said. "That's it, a little closer."

Cali felt heady, enveloped by Ethan's scent. So warm and full of spice. And then she felt one of his hands slip around her waist and linger at her hipbone. The blood climbed into her cheeks.

He leaned close enough so only she could hear. "You're going to make it impossible to think about stray cats tonight," he murmured, his voice low and a little rougher than he intended.

Her mouth curved in that small, knowing smile. And just as she was about to offer a witty remark, the camera light flashed.

"Got it," Minka said cheerily. "Okay, see ya!"

She started backing away from them, but Cali saw the wet, dreamy glow in her eyes. She mouthed *Traitor* at Minka, which only made Minka's grin widen.

Ethan released her hip and glanced down at her. "Remind me," he said lightly, playfully, his lips mere inches from hers, "are you here to help the cats or ruin every man who gets within ten feet of you?"

Cali laughed nervously. "So I wanted to go look at some of the things up for auction. I'll be back before the doors open." She turned and dashed off, pretending she didn't feel his gaze tracing her every step. She wasn't sure which unnerved her more—that he was watching or that she didn't want him to stop.

Chapter 24

The hum of preparation filled the ballroom again—silverware clinking, hushed laughter from the kitchen doors, someone testing the mic near the stage. Cali slowed her pace between the tables, studying the handwritten bid cards while her pulse worked to steady itself. The tables gleamed under the chandelier light, a patchwork of generosity and small-town pride—baskets of wine, vouchers for spa days, a birdhouse she was ninety percent certain had been repurposed from one of Russell's craft-night disasters at the library.

"Thank God for bad decoupage," she muttered under her breath.

So many stories were tucked into each item. But the one that stopped her was a small oak wood box at the far end of the table, its lid carved with the image of two cats sitting yin-yang style, one light wood color and one dark from the stain. They had button noses and their whiskers were so finely carved. She wanted to touch it, but the displays instructed them not to. The dovetail lid was pushed to one side. No donor name. So it was one of the three anonymous donations Ethan had secured. Just a note that read *Hand-crafted. One of a kind.*

Cali imagined her grandmother's heirloom jewelry nestled inside it or maybe Charley's old collar and tag, which were currently in a plastic bag of keepsakes in her closet. Both the jewelry and collar deserved more, and the box was worthy of display on any of her shelves.

Then again, there was also a photo of a gorgeous wooden porch swing a few displays down. But the starting bid was out of her reach, and she didn't know how on earth she'd get it down to the lake house anyway.

She glanced over her shoulder and caught Ethan sitting by the front doors, his eyes still locked on her.

A loud whistle sounded from the center of the ballroom. "Places," Mrs. Ellery instructed them. "We're about to open, and it looks like all of Autumn Ridge is on the other side of that door. You ready, Lynne?" she shouted toward the bar.

Lynne gave her a thumbs up.

"Mayor Pennington and sound crew?"

The folks on the stage hooted and hollered.

Cali scurried back to Ethan's side in the nick of time.

"Cali and Ethan?"

"Ready, Mrs. E," Ethan called back.

Then the hotel staff opened the doors. It was a flurry of activity of both Cali and Ethan for nearly forty-five minutes straight, and they danced around each other as they collected coats and passed out tickets. Each time she felt concern over the line backing up, Ethan picked up his pace or reminded her that sometimes waiting for things only made people want them more. When he thought he'd forgotten to collect the entrance fee from a couple people, Cali was quick to point out each one of them were either likely to bid big tonight anyway or should be an exception to the rule—long-time residents who'd already helped them with the cat searches. By the end of the hour, they were more than just volunteers. They were a team.

Cali noticed, at one point, several men from Ethan's construction crew showed up as well. The switch from construction hats to suits made them all act different, except Carl. Carl heckled Ethan, and while Ethan fell into brief conversation with the guys, Carl leaned down to take his drink tickets from Cali.

"We told him we came to win one of those gift cards for Sutton's Auto Body since we didn't win anything back at the festival," he explained to her. "But the Mayor actually invited us for some kind of send-off." His expression turned very serious then. "Hey. Shhh. Don't tell him I told you that, okay? The crew will kill me."

Her brow furrowed in confusion. But Carl, being Carl, failed to notice. He told the guys to get a move on, and they headed toward the auction displays as one big, uncomfortable pile of polyester.

Cali couldn't help but notice, as the line thinned out and the interior of the ballroom bloomed with noise and motion, how many people had personally greeted Ethan at the door. Handshakes and thank you's sprinkled every round of small talk, and it occurred to her Ethan hadn't just been building Mrs. Ellery's gazebo or Bernadette's cat tower recently. He'd been rebuilding the whole town.

When the last coat was collected and the last ticket passed out, the hotel staff closed the doors and offered Cali and Ethan some hors d'oeuvres. Minka swung around for some final candid pics with The Nine, and everyone took a seat. Cali and Ethan hung out together in the back of the room, watching Mayor Pennington sashay up on stage and give her introduction for the event.

"Good evening, Autumn Ridge! Thank you all for coming out tonight to support our four-legged residents and the two-legged heroes who help them. I see some familiar faces here, and a few I only recognize from the comments on Minka's social media posts."

Ethan and Cali turned to each other and giggled just as the crowd joined in. Mayor Pennington paused for Minka to snap another picture from below the stage.

"Tonight's gala is about more than fancy outfits and bidding wars. Though I'll be honest, I'm *very* curious to see which of our fine firefighters earns the highest bid."

She winked at Leo, and Leo blew the crowd a kiss.

"Such a showman," Cali whispered, as the hearts of every single lady and man in Autumn Ridge in that room skipped a beat.

Mayor Pennington continued. "It's about giving our town's strays a shot at a home, a belly full of food, and the love every creature deserves. Since we don't have a shelter, you all make that possible. So thank you for being the heart of this community." She motioned for the three firefighters to come to the front of the stage. "Alright, folks. Now for the moment half of Autumn Ridge has been waiting for and the other half's been pretending not to... the firefighter date auction!" Everyone clapped as Leo stepped forward. One woman at a table in the middle whistled. "Starting off strong with Leo March here. You know him. You've probably called him to save a kitten from a tree, and now's your chance to thank him personally over dinner. Rumor has it he can operate a grill without setting off the alarms. Bidding starts at fifty dollars, and remember, this is a *date*—not a house call. The department has enough of those already."

"Fifty dollars!" Russell screamed from the library staff's table. The crowd practically fell over with laughter.

The Mayor leaned into the mic again. "Gentle reminder to use the paddles at your tables, please." Her eyes flitted to the library's table. "Russ, I'm sure it's not the first time someone's asked you that politely." A low rumble of laughter. "Joking. Joking. But remember folks, if the bidders get too wild, we *will* call in Animal Control."

As the bids quickly escalated, Cali noticed some playful heckling.

"I'll bid if he brings his older brother!"

"Does the date come with dessert?"

One elderly woman seemed to be bidding purely to make her bridge club jealous.

When she wondered why she hadn't seen Lynne's hand fly up yet, she glanced over at the bar and caught her mouthing *Don't you dare* at Minka. But Lynne did eventually raise her paddle when the numbers got good and high but started to stall.

The elderly—and now tipsy—woman who'd been trying to impress her bridge club yelled, "Four hundred!" and the crowd cheered. But Lynne called her bluff.

"Four hundred fifty," Lynne countered, hiding her grin behind her champagne glass.

"Five hundred!"

"Six!"

"Seven!"

Lynne kept her paddle to herself.

The room roared with laughter and applause as Mayor Pennington leaned into the mic. "Well! Our firefighters may put out flames, but apparently, they're starting a few tonight," she teased. "Mrs. McAllister, I expect pictures—and a chaperone."

Lynne raised her hand again, eyes twinkling. "Eight-fifty."

The older woman gasped, then lifted her paddle one last time.

CHAPTER 24

"Nine hundred!"

"Going once. Going twice. Sold!" Mayor Pennington cried, banging the gavel she'd somehow acquired for the occasion. "To Mrs. McAllister! Come collect your prize beside the stage. Next firefighter, please." She turned to Mrs. Ellery behind her and squealed, "I didn't realize this would be so much fun!"

Ethan leaned toward Cali, their arms touching, as the switch to the next auction item happened. "Did anything catch your eye?" he asked. "You bidding tonight?"

"A little something," she whispered. "I really wanted that porch swing, but there's no way to get it home." Before he offered to cart it there for her, she added, "Plus I can't really afford it, *and* it seems to be the talk of the night. Outside of Leo. But if everything goes like Leo's auction, I may not even win my second pick." She sighed. "But that's okay. It's all for the cats."

"I doubt every item is as hot as Leo," Ethan quipped. "What else do you want?"

Cali hesitated. She felt like if she shared, Ethan would do something chivalrous, like try to win it for her. "Promise you won't bid on it if I start losing, just to make me feel better," she said.

Ethan grinned. "You know me too well. But sure, if that's what you want."

"Okay, so there was a little keepsake box with a top that slides open."

"The one with the cats carved on it?"

"Yes, exactly. I'd love to have that, whether it's for Charley's old collar or some of my grandmother's jewelry."

"Sounds perfect," he said.

Cali side-eyed him. "Don't bid on it."

"I said I wouldn't." He scoffed, still smiling.

They pushed through most of the items up for auction, with the biggest bids going to the porch swing, just as Cali suspected, and a beautiful farmhouse dining table—won by Mr. Winslow, the owner of Candlewick Orchard. Cali swore she caught Minka glancing around the room in a panic, searching for his son Grady. But just as soon as the thought registered, Minka was behind her phone again.

Finally, just when Cali thought they might have forgotten about it, the auction for the keepsake cat box started. She won it easily, as by that time most of the town had already spent its money and enthusiasm on other items up for auction.

"I guess you didn't have to warn me not to rescue after all," Ethan commented.

"No, but one can never be too careful. You've got a habit of rescuing things that don't need saving," she reminded him.

The crowd hushed, and Mrs. Ellery and some of The Nine gathered behind the mayor on stage. Mrs. Ellery took the microphone. "I have some excellent news for you all. The official numbers are in. Tonight's grand total will fund 30 stray cats from intake to adoption. That's approximately 85 months of foster care for anyone in Autumn Ridge willing to open up their home to foster. Food, litter, meds, vet visits—the Nine Lives Club can now cover all of that." The crowd cheered. Cali leapt to her feet in surprise. Mrs. Ellery waited for everyone to settle before she went on. "In plain terms, this fundraiser was a huge success. Every bid tonight turned into full bellies, vet visits, and safe sleeps. So if you see a stray cat, please tag us on social media using one of Minka's hashtags or call me or the Autumn Ridge library and ask for Cali Jacobs. Let any one of us know, and we'll rally to get it some shelter and food."

CHAPTER 24

More clapping, more cheering. The town's enthusiasm for their win seemed to match the enthusiasm of The Nine.

"Congrats, congrats!" the mayor said, taking the microphone again. "Before we leave, may I also say a few more words? You all know how much I love to do it."

A few heckles came from the crowd, but everyone remained seated as waitstaff rushed in to collect empty dishes and glasses. Next thing she knew, Carl was screaming "Do it, Mayor!" at the stage, and all of Ethan's coworkers were on their feet and clapping.

Mayor Pennington grinned so big her eyes disappeared behind her glasses. "Ethan, can you come to the stage?" she asked.

Ethan pointed at himself, perplexed. He glanced over at Cali, and she shrugged her shoulders at him. Her stomach dropped as she watched him shuffle up to the stage, remembering what Carl said about Ethan's "send-off." Maybe the mayor was giving him some sort of medal or key to the city before they left for the next construction project. Her eyes searched the room for Minka, wondering if she had the heart to stick around for this part. Then the mayor started in on another speech.

"I first met Ethan Cross when he offered to build a bench for our cemetery to memorialize Autumn Ridge's fallen soldiers," Mayor Pennington started. "Ethan's stepdad is a veteran, and Ethan and his crew have been fixing more than City Hall this year. They've been rebuilding the heart of this town. Ethan, specifically, has been rebuilding community spirit by rolling up his sleeves to fix everything under the sun. So the city council thought it was only right he get to roll out his new business in style."

Behind them, on a screen, someone projected an image.

Ethan turned around and saw a large white cargo van with the name "Crosstown Repairs" emblazoned on the side, parked in front of City Hall with the Mayor waving beside it.

"We're so happy you decided to stay and be part of this community, Ethan. That van will get one more tune up and meet you at City Hall on Monday."

"Woohoo!" Carl screamed, his face nearly red. Cali couldn't help but laugh at his unbridled joy. "Come here! Come here!" he called up to Ethan, and as he stepped down, the guys all huddled around him, football-style.

"And while we're at it," the mayor continued, "because there's no community without compassion—The Nine will also be getting a new transport van for their furry rescues, courtesy of the council."

Another picture appeared with a similar van with "The Nine Lives Rescue Squad" written on it, decked in paw prints. Mrs. Ellery was behind the wheel in that photo. Cali gasped and covered her mouth. Her eyes first met with Minka, then almost all of The Nine found each other's startled faces in the crowd. "Thanks to Mrs. Ellery for keeping our secret. We couldn't imagine this place without you all."

The applause built until it felt like the whole ballroom was vibrating. Cali clapped until her palms stung, but even that couldn't shake the tightness in her throat. She'd spent the past couple years watching people leave Autumn Ridge, chasing bigger, louder lives—and now here was Ethan, choosing to stay. For once, it felt like the town was giving something back, not taking it away.

Beside her, Leo appeared, wiping at his eyes with the corner of a cocktail napkin, muttering something about allergies. Minka was next to him, grabbing Cali's hand like a kid spotting Santa.

CHAPTER 24

Ethan broke away from his cheering crew and made his way toward them through the crowd. When he reached Leo, the two pulled each other into a full-bodied hug that made the room erupt all over again.

"Hands off my firefighter!" someone shouted through the noise.

"Before you all head out, we have one more surprise. If you'll follow us out to the parking lot, Autumn Ridge has something sparkly to say thank you."

Mrs. Ellery leaned toward the mic with a grin. "And this way, we can clear the ballroom before anyone gets into a fight over the firefighters."

Laughter rippled through the crowd. The trio turned toward Lynne, who was scowling behind the bar. Leo frowned and cleared his throat.

Cali leaned closer to Ethan and whispered, "The running joke is that Mayor Pennington keeps getting re-elected because she'll set off fireworks for any and every reason."

Ethan grinned down at her. "That's my kind of Mayor."

"I think that's my cue to leave," Leo huffed. "You guys still coming out to O'Donnell's for my birthday? Halloween night?" Cali and Ethan nodded. "Catch you there then. This smoke is bound to set off some false alarms throughout town." His phone rang then—a desperate, angry voice on the other end of the line. "I swear it's just smoke, Chief," they heard him say as he slipped through the ballroom doors. "I know. Happens every time. But I'm headed to the firehouse now."

The rest of The Nine and some of Cali's library staff did offer to help with coats so everyone could watch the fireworks together. In no time the crowd was spilling into the parking lot, calling names, waving to neighbors. Cali lost track of Ethan as she grabbed her coat and purse and the wave of people pushed her beyond the hotel doors.

Chapter 25

Outside, the fairy lights gave way to the cool dark sky. The crowd spilled into the parking lot like a river of sequins and chatter. Mayor Pennington's voice carried over the murmur—cheerful and practiced.

"As promised, one last surprise for our guests! Please keep a safe distance from the launch site, and thank you for helping make Autumn Ridge shine tonight!"

Cali tugged her coat tighter as the first rocket screamed upward. It burst into a pale gold bloom, then another and another, until the sky above the Inn glowed in mirrored flashes on every car hood. The noise filled her chest in that bittersweet way joy sometimes does. Loud and bright and almost too much to hold.

Ethan found her in the crowd and tipped his head toward his truck parked beyond the crowd.

"Best view's back here," he said.

She followed him, and they climbed up into his truck bed together, side by side, the metal cool beneath them. Around them, the town cheered at each burst of color, mirrored against two new, glossy vans parked in the parking lot. Cali rested her chin on her knees and let the wind from the explosions lift strands of her hair.

"You did good tonight," Ethan said softly. "The whole town's talking about The Nine now."

"*We* did good," she corrected.

He smiled, then nodded toward the keepsake box resting beside her. "Why don't you look inside?"

Cali hesitated then picked it up, fingers brushing the carved lid. Inside, the box smelled faintly of woodsmoke and varnish. The fireworks popped overhead—red, white, gold—as her eyes caught something carved at the base. *E C.*

Her breath caught as the pieces fell into place. She gazed up at him, but he was watching the sky, its reflection flickering in his gray eyes.

"You made this," she whispered. "And all of those anonymous donations were yours?"

He didn't answer, just reached across the space between them and twined his fingers with hers. Another firework bloomed, silver this time, bright enough to paint both of them in its glow.

"Looks like the Mayor's going for another re-election," Ethan murmured.

Cali laughed, cozy and tired and happy all at once. "She'll win by a landslide."

A final flare of gold spiraled upward and broke open into a thousand glittering embers. The crowd cheered somewhere beyond them, but neither of them moved. They sat that way until the last sparkle died out, relishing the warmth of each other's hand, his thumb brushing along hers.

When Cali's phone vibrated in her purse, she glanced at the screen and saw a message from Minka. *Headed home. Ethan said he'd drive you back.* A bunch of silly-faced emojis and hearts followed.

She turned to Ethan, heart still thudding from the fireworks.

"Truth or kiss," she said softly. "Why didn't you just tell me you had plans to stay in Autumn Ridge?"

He let out a small laugh—half sigh, half surrender. "Because I didn't have plans," he admitted. "Not really. I figured I'd finish the job, pocket the check, and move on—same as always. Then somewhere along the way, I started thinking maybe I could stick around a little longer. The side work was steady, the people were kind, and for once it didn't feel like I was just passing through someone else's life. I thought maybe that was enough."

He looked out toward the empty lot where the last threads of the smoke curled into the sky.

"And then I saw you outside the library that morning, feeding the stray cats. You were just standing there in the sun, completely unaware that you were about to rearrange my life. It wasn't just that you looked like you belonged here—it was that, for the first time in a long time, I wanted to belong somewhere, too. With you. And I had to figure it out before Carl hauled me to the next town. No plan. Lease running out. Time slipping right along with it."

Cali swallowed. "But I didn't make it easy for you. I kept pulling back."

Ethan nodded once. "I know." His voice lowered as he met her eyes again. "But once I realized I could actually see myself building something that lasts—with *you*—I had to keep trying. Every time I networked, or stayed up late, or traded fixes for cookies instead of money, you were on my mind. Does that make sense?"

She nodded, her throat tight.

"Good," he murmured. "Because if it's all the same to you, I choose the kiss."

She slid closer, cupping his jaw in her hands until he drew his lips to hers. Their mouths kept finding each other, soft and unhurried. Each return was more certain, like they'd finally stopped fighting gravity.

He rubbed his cold nose against hers. "Ready to head out?"

She was teary, relieved, half-laughing from adrenaline. "My place or yours?"

"Ladies choice."

She bit her lip, remembering Max's soft fur and the purrs he'd bestowed on her in bed last time he was at her place. "Can I... see them?" she asked. "Then maybe my place."

Ethan understood. "I'll do you one better. Let's swing by my place, pick up the fur kids, and we'll all spend the night at your house."

"That sounds great," Cali said. "I want Max home. I want you there, too."

"And we know Catsby won't care either way as long as she's still in charge." He slid down from the bed and offered to help her down. "Let's go home."

Back at Ethan's townhome, they found the cats curled together on the couch. Catsby gave them slow blinks and Max stretched, but neither budged. When Cali pulled cat treats from her purse, they were easily lured into their carriers, though.

They pulled up to the A-frame to the sound of hooting owls and the squeak of her neighbor's weather vane in the night wind.

Ethan carried the cats' carriers inside, set them down, and released their doors. Max and Catsby went scurrying off, one after the other, toward the loft room.

"I'm sure Max will let her know all the good places to sleep," Cali said, adjusting the lights and slipping off her coat.

CHAPTER 25

Ethan glanced around the kitchen. "Still feels weird seeing this place so quiet," he said.

"Quiet?" she asked.

"Yeah. No wine bottles, no pots and pans. No you, sitting on this countertop, driving me insane."

Her lips curved as she stepped closer to him. "Well, we could fix that."

He looked at her for a moment then lifted her onto the countertop. She squealed with delight as he traced eager kisses along her collarbone.

"Shall we pick up where we left off?" he asked.

He undid his tie, and a thrill ran up her spine. "No. This round deserves the bedroom. Follow me."

She took his hands in hers and guided him to the door nearest the bathroom, shutting it behind them. Ethan paused to take in the ambience, the bedroom's simple colors and dim lamplight. It smelled of fresh linen and her. Her clothes, her perfume, her everything.

He pulled her close, and their mouths met over and over. Each time was unique, like a snowflake, like no matter how they tried to kiss, it crystallized then melted into the next. Cali could feel the gnawing heat grow in her stomach again. As if on command, one of her straps fell from her shoulder, and Ethan filled the space with his lips, planting light kisses along her collarbone and sucking gently at the base of her neck. Her skin tingled at the sensation.

"I wasn't ready to see you like this," he confessed. "The minute you walked into that ballroom, I lost all restraint."

He grasped the other strap in his hand and slid the dress off her. Then he stood before her, speechless, as he admired the matching red strapless bra and seamless panties.

"You enjoy driving me crazy, don't you?"

She nodded her head and slipped his gray blazer off and lifted her hands to the collar of his button-down shirt. "So many buttons," she teased, undoing each one and kissing down his sternum and abdomen as she did it. She sat on the bed in front of him, legs parted, and glided her hands around the back of his trousers. She pulled his pelvis closer to her, the swell of him unmistakable through the fabric of his pants. Ethan dug into his pocket and placed a condom on the nightstand beside the bed.

She glanced up at him, their eyes meeting.

"You don't have to," he said.

"But I want to."

She grasped the zipper between her delicate fingers, pulled down, and guided his pants to the floor. He stepped out of the legs, kicked them off to the side, and she admired how his body moved under her touch. Jaw grinding. Hands fisted then relaxed. The deep V of muscle along his abdomen a tight line that disappeared into his briefs. He was nearly naked, vulnerable, barely able to contain himself. As she held his gaze, he ran fingers through her hair and along her chin.

"Okay," he said, "but don't take me over the edge. I can't get your words from the other night out of my head, Cali. In my truck. In the rain." His cheeks went ruddy. "I want to be inside of you, too."

She ran a hand along the band of his underwear and slipped them off as well. He shuddered as her breath ghosted over his skin. Her touch turned deliberate—a blend of delicate nibbles and licks, then slowly lavishing him until a low sound drew from deep in his chest. Each tremble of his body was its own delicious reward.

CHAPTER 25

"That feels so damn good," Ethan said breathlessly.

"You think you can handle more?"

"Oh, I'm not done with you yet."

He hooked an arm around her waist and lifted her into the center of the plush bedding. She giggled at how effortless he made it feel.

Within moments her bra and panties were off, and Ethan was showering her with caresses. The space between them vanished, replaced by the sound of breath and the slide of skin. Like an orchestra, he played and fiddled and hummed in smooth, swelling motions. Her body swayed to the beat he crafted, their breathing steady, syncopated, real. Then he reached for protection, rolled the condom on, and pushed into her, slow and deliberate, until she gasped and arched against him. A mix of agony and pleasure unfolded, their rhythm building together until the rest of the world fell away. Her edges blurred. She couldn't tell where her body ended and his began, or whether it was his pulse or hers echoing through the quiet.

She came first, but the sound of her crying out his name made him come soon after. When he finished, she pressed her forehead to his, breath still trembling between them. For the first time in weeks, she didn't feel caught between wanting and resisting. She was just here, now, his warmth anchoring her.

"You okay?" he murmured. He brushed a stray curl from her cheek, his thumb catching the corner of her smile.

"Better than okay."

They stayed tangled in the hush that followed, their breaths slowing in unison.

"I should've gone for the box *and* the porch swing," she said playfully.

"Don't worry. I'll build you a porch swing, too."

He planted a kiss on her temple and reached to turn off the lamp. As the lamplight faded, Cali thought of the night sky over Autumn Ridge—the fireworks, the laughter, the way everything that mattered had come home. The room fell into soft darkness all around them. Outside, the fall wind rustled through the trees, but inside, she finally felt still.

Chapter 26

Cali woke to the smell of coffee brewing and something warm and sugary. When she turned over, she realized Ethan wasn't beside her. Instead, Catsby was curled against the pillow where his head had been, and Max was tucked at her feet, purring softly into the comforter. She stretched, then reached for Ethan's dress shirt on the floor, wrapping his scent around her as she buttoned it up.

"Good morning," she said, padding into the kitchen and perching on one of the high-top chairs. "Whatcha making?"

"Pancakes." He glanced over his shoulder, wearing nothing but his underwear—and for a moment, Cali had to remind herself how to breathe. "Simple, I know. But then I realized you had all these apples, and your apple pie spices were still sitting out. So I folded some grated apple into the pancake mix and used the rest for a warm topping. Should be ready in just a bit."

She got up, kissed his cheek, and let her fingertips linger on the dip of muscle just above his waistband. He set the spatula down, turned, and kissed her back—deeply enough to kick up her pulse.

"You look cute in my shirt," he whispered, trying to restrain himself. "But if you touch me like that again before we eat, I might burn breakfast."

"Wouldn't want that," she whispered back. "But how about some coffee first?" She reached past him for the drip pot.

"Already on it." He jutted his chin toward the opposite counter, where a homemade version of her favorite Oat Couture latte sat, steam curling up from the rim.

She took a sip as he finished, the scent of cinnamon and butter filling the kitchen.

This was just what she'd hoped for, what she imagined it could be. Slow Sunday mornings, him cooking a delicious breakfast, the cats lounging in the sunlight as it scattered through the windows. Who knew what else they might stir up together today? They had all the time in the world now. Together. She bit her lip imagining it.

What amazed her most wasn't just how right it felt, but how easy. How the idea of belonging—and trusting she was wanted—no longer scared her at all.

Catsby suddenly got the zoomies, and Max chased after her, the two playing like they'd been littermates from the start.

Ethan sauntered over to the table and set down their pancakes, warm and golden and glistening with syrup. Almost too good to cut into. As they ate, they reminisced about the gala and Ethan's growing list of handyman requests around town. Cali told him about the upcoming Twelve Books of Christmas reading festival and how it was Russell's and Bernadette's turn to dress as Mr. and Mrs. Claus. Though this year, they were switching it up—her in a sparkly red suit and him as a snowflake. Cali would start their measurements next week.

When Ethan finished his last bite of pancake, he reached for a measuring tape sitting among the mugs and spices.

"Where on earth did you get that?" she asked. "Do those

things just follow you?"

He grinned, kneeling by the window as the tape snapped open.

"Oh, no," she said. "Please tell me you didn't find something else to fix already. I'll be embarrassed—or you'll have to start charging overtime."

"Nope. Just seeing where a second cat tower might fit. Looks like there's room for two right here."

"But what if we get more cats?" she teased.

"Guess we'll have to keep measuring," he said, tugging her close. "Are you done with those pancakes already or what?"

She placed one more bite in her mouth, savoring it, chewing slowly while holding his gaze. Then she put her fork down. "Done."

He scooped her into his arms and buried his face against her neck as she let out a delighted laugh.

"Finally," he said.

"You mean breakfast or me?"

"Both," he murmured, kissing her again.

Epilogue

One year later ...

Autumn had returned to Autumn Ridge, all burnished gold and woodsmoke and the rustle of leaves along the porch. The swing Ethan had once promised now hung beneath the eaves, built from scratch and stained to match the deck. It swayed lazily in the breeze with the two of them nestled on its cushion, the sliding glass door open behind them, the whole house smelling faintly of coffee, sawdust, and home.

Catsby snored from her perch on the second cat tower just inside. Max blinked sleepily from Cali's lap. And somewhere in the kitchen, Ethan's phone kept pinging with new repair requests for Crosstown Repairs. Carl and Ethan's old coworkers had been keeping in touch, even though their current worksite was in California, with hopes for a guys' weekend sometime next year.

This would be the second Autumn for Ethan, fourth for Cali. Minka was already making plans with them to pick apples at Candlewick, and they'd spotted the crew members setting up the Ferris wheel for the fall festival last time Ethan dropped Cali off at the library for work.

The year had been full of memories for the four of them. The holidays with her family. Now her brother and Ethan were like best friends—constantly texting each other, trading advice, debating the latest scores. She'd nursed Ethan through a terrible flu in the spring, and he'd done the same for her. They went fishing with Leo in the summer—though Cali preferred reading on the dock. No more furry escape artistry, but The Nine had helped them celebrate another year around the sun for both Catsby and Max. It was almost too good to be true. A year full of Sundays just like the first one they'd shared. Her heart swelled just thinking about it.

The porch swing rocked in an easy rhythm as they read the latest book club pick together, the wood creaking against the hush of evening. Ethan set down his book and slipped his arm around her shoulders, coffee mug balanced in his other hand. Across the lake, the sun melted into pink and gold.

"The swing is perfect," she said. "But you do realize this is technically the fourth thing you've built me this year."

He smiled. "Promised I'd get around to it. Hope the wait was worth it." He kissed her cheek. "Love you."

Those words still wrapped her in warmth, better than any blanket, no matter how many times he'd said them. "Love you, too. And, yes, worth every second. You finished it just in time for cozy blankets and watching the leaves change. My favorite season."

"I remember." He shuddered a little and pulled his hand through his hair. Speaking of ... do you feel that chill?"

Cali nodded, and he ducked inside to grab the largest, plushest throw from their blanket basket. When he returned, he lifted Max from her lap, cradling him as he draped half the blanket over her. Then he settled Max back down and slipped beneath the softness beside them both. She felt his skin and warmth and spicy scent pressing against her own.

When she turned toward him, he reached into his pocket and

held out a small, sanded-wood box between them. No velvet, no shine.

"You made this?" she whispered, brushing her thumb over the smooth wood. "Another keepsake box? It's beautiful."

"Same wood as your deck," he said softly. "Seemed fitting. But it's not exactly a keepsake box. Go ahead—open it."

Inside was a curved wood-inlay ring with a tension-set gem that caught the last of the sunset.

The corners of his mouth turned up. "You're everything I've ever wanted, Cali. You don't just feel like home. You *are* home. Will you marry me?"

Her throat tightened, eyes blurring. "You're impossible. You know that?"

He lifted a brow. "Is that a yes?"

"An enthusiastic yes," she said, grinning as he slipped the ring onto her finger.

Max batted at her hand, the sparkle of the ring catching his attention. Cali laughed. "Hey, bubs! That's mine." She stroked his head until he purred.

The porch swing rocked, the cats settled, and for the first time, home wasn't a place—it was a person. Cali squeezed Ethan's hand and sighed. "Guess love at first scratch really does exist."

Before You Go ...

If this story made you smile, swoon, or reach for your own cat, please consider leaving a review where you purchased the book. Even a few words make a huge difference in helping more readers find their next happily-ever-after. Thanks for supporting indie romance!

Soundtrack for Love at First Scratch

Check out the "Love at First Scratch" public playlist created by Hazel Mayes on Spotify or recreate it wherever you enjoy music.

1. "Cruel Summer" – Taylor Swift
2. "Bloom" – The Paper Kites
3. "Light On" – Maggie Rogers
4. "Eugene" – Arlo Parks
5. "Geronimo" – Sheppard
6. "Fresh Eyes" – Andy Grammer
7. "Slow Burn" – Kacey Musgraves
8. "Damn I Wish I Was Your Lover" – Sophie B. Hawkins
9. "Ceilings" – Lizzy McAlpine
10. "Breathe Again" – Joy Oladokun
11. "Outnumbered" – Dermot Kennedy
12. "I'm With You" – Avril Lavigne
13. "Evergreen" – Yebba
14. "Next to Me" – Sleeping at Last
15. "Carry Me Home" – Jorja Smith & Maverick Sabre
16. "The Few Things" – JP Saxe
17. "Home" – JOHNNYSWIM

Cats Who Inspired the Story

Every book in the *Nine Lives Club* series has a little real-life feline magic behind it. This one belongs to my cat **Max**, a Maine Coon who showed up on my back porch as a kitten after his mother (whom I'd been feeding in the hopes of TNR) disappeared. With a heart as big as Autumn Ridge itself, Max's love of cuddles and quiet loyalty inspired this story's four-legged matchmaker.

Our heroine is also a tribute to my cat **Cali**, who passed unexpectedly in June 2025. Though she was the youngest in the house, she was easily the wittiest and sassiest of the bunch. Writing *Love at First Scratch* has been my way of processing that loss and keeping Cali—and all our cats, past and present—close to my heart.

Join the Series!

Hey, reader! Want your cat to inspire a future *Nine Lives Club* story? Tag me in their photo **@authorhazelmayes** on Instagram and tell me a little about them—their quirks, how you met, or what makes them unforgettable. Yours might just become the next furry matchmaker in Autumn Ridge.

A Note from Hazel

Every cat deserves a safe place to land. If you've enjoyed this book from the *Nine Lives Club* series, please consider donating to your local shelter or national organizations like the ASPCA, the International Fund for Animal Welfare, Best Friends Animal Society, or Alley Cat Allies.

Love always finds a way—sometimes on four paws (or three or two).

Book Club Discussion Guide

Love at First Scratch **(Book #1 of the *Nine Lives Club* series)**

1. Every book in the *Nine Lives Club* starts with one of the Club's tongue-in-cheek "Rules." If you were to write your own Rule for a future romance with the Nine Lives Club, what would it be?
2. Both Cali and Ethan start the story feeling a little unmoored. How do their ideas of "home" change over the course of the book? Did either of their journeys toward belonging resonate with your own?
3. In what ways does Autumn Ridge itself serve as a place for second chances, both for people and for animals? How do the strays mirror the human characters' stories?
4. Cali and Ethan's connection grows through a series of small, vulnerable moments, not grand gestures. Which scene felt like the *turning point* for their relationship, and why?
5. How do Cali and Ethan express care for each other — through words, acts of service, humor, or physical touch? Do you think they'd score similarly on a "love languages" quiz?
6. What did you enjoy most about the dynamic of The Nine? Who stood out to you, and why? If you could volunteer

alongside one of them, who would it be?
7. At the start, Ethan assumes he's just "passing through," and Cali assumes she's too guarded for love. How do those self-perceptions hold them back? And what finally breaks through those walls?
8. From Max to Catsby, the animals are more than background characters. They often *catalyze* change. Which feline moment stole your heart or made you laugh the most?
9. The Autumn Ridge gala brought the whole town together for a shared cause. How does that scene reflect the larger spirit of the book? And what does it say about how love and generosity ripple through a small town?
10. Which side characters are you most excited to see again in future books? (Lynne and Leo, perhaps?) What are your predictions for how the *Nine Lives Club* will continue to grow, and who might fall in love next?

Bonus Prompt: "Love at first scratch" can mean finding connection in the most unexpected place, even after life's bruises. What was your favorite 'scratch' moment in the story—a small act that left a lasting mark?

About the Author

Hazel Mayes pens the *Nine Lives Club* series—a cozy-with-heat romance collection where the town's cats have as much matchmaking talent as the locals. Expect heart, humor, and just enough spice to keep things interesting. Hazel lives with a revolving cast of rescued felines who are convinced they're her co-authors.

Social: https://www.instagram.com/authorhazelmayes/

Web: https://hazelmayes.my.canva.site/

Newsletter: https://hazelmayes.substack.com/

Also by Hazel Mayes

Hot Under the Collar, the next book in the *Nine Lives Club* series, turns up the heat with a second-chance romance that refuses to stay buried. Coming in late 2026 ...

Hot Under the Collar

Years ago, on Leo March's twenty-first birthday, one reckless night rewired everything between him and Lynne O'Donnell. Now, when Lynne discovers a litter of kittens and their feral mom inside her bar, all signs point to Leo's wandering tomcat as the culprit. Suddenly they're stuck co-parenting fluffballs, dodging town gossip, and bumping into every piece of unresolved history they've tried to avoid. With the kittens trapping them back in each other's orbit, Lynne and Leo have to decide: keep circling the same old patterns or admit the fire between them never went out.

www.ingramcontent.com/pod-product-compliance
Lightning Source LLC
LaVergne TN
LVHW041932070526
838199LV00051BA/2779